When Westram McKinley met Noah Redruvian, an uncouth offer for a roll in the hay has Noah painting him with the same brush as his ex-boyfriend — an unfaithful playboy. As a nearly two-century-old longnose saw-shark shifter, he did have plenty of experience, but nothing could have been further from the truth. Noah was his mate. Westram would never stray from the man. As weeks without his mate turn into months, Westram's shark begins to pine, becoming increasingly volatile, only calmed with the help of his alpha, Kaiser. The continued updates about Noah from Kaiser's mate, Arthur — who is good buddies with the man — also help keep Westram from losing his mind. When Arthur comes to Westram and shares that Noah hasn't answered his calls in two days, Westram doesn't waste a second. He heads to Noah's, ready for any type of vitriol the distrustful human throws at him. To his dismay, when he arrives, Noah is injured and nearly catatonic, fear oozing from every pore. Can Westram figure out how to soothe Noah and get his mate to talk to him before whatever danger had terrorized him returns?

Snorkeling with a Saw-shark
Copyright © 2020 Charlie Richards
ISBN: 978-1-4874-3166-2
Cover art by Angela Waters

Published by eXtasy Books Inc or
Devine Destinies, an imprint of eXtasy Books Inc

Look for us online at:
www.eXtasybooks.com or www.devinedestinies.com

Snorkeling with a Saw-shark Beneath Aquatica's Waves Book Nine

By

Charlie Richards

DEDICATION

Sweet Serendipity . . . that unexpected meeting that changes your life.
~Alexia

CHAPTER ONE

Westram McKinley strolled slowly through his assigned section of the *World of Aquatica* marine park. While his gaze strayed over everything around him, his mind wasn't on his job. It was a good thing just the presence of a man in a security uniform dissuaded most from trying anything because Westram would surely have missed anyone actually doing something wrong.

Instead, just as it had been for the last couple of months, Westram's mind was firmly fixed on his mate — Noah Redruvian. He longed to pull the sweet-smelling and cute-as-hell human into his arms. He wanted to taste his full lips and squeeze his plump ass.

Too bad Westram didn't see that happening anytime soon.

All because of one thoughtless comment.

When Westram had first met Noah, he'd been there in a guard capacity. A stalker had been after Arthur, his alpha's mate. They'd chosen a plan to lure the man out. That created danger for Arthur's friends, too.

Westram had been assigned to Noah, while Dare — a fellow shifter enforcer — had been ordered to watch Arthur's other best friend, Jacob. Walking into the house where the pair waited — Arthur had wanted to explain the situation first — had been the most surreal and magical moment of Westram's nearly two-century life.

Then Jacob had opened his big mouth, starting a chain reaction that caused Westram to mentally cringe any time he thought about it.

"Mmm," Jacob had purred, eyeing Dare like a tasty steak. "If you're gonna be my bodyguard, big guy, I guess I don't have a problem with it." Jacob had extended his hand to him.

Dare had grinned broadly as he'd reached out and wrapped his large dark hand around Jacob's much smaller one. Using the hold, he'd tugged the human close while saying, "Does that mean you'd be amenable to recreating a scene or two from *The Bodyguard*?"

Resting his free hand on Dare's chest, Jacob grinned up at him, obvious heat in his green eyes. "Oh, definitely."

Growling softly, Dare lowered his head, placing his lips close to Jacob's ear. "I look forward to that."

Westram would forever blame his behavior on the pheromones the pair were pumping out.

Fixing his gaze on Noah, Westram had skimmed the backs of his forefingers down his arm. "What about you, handsome?" he asked, his voice husky with need. Reaching Noah's hand, he slid his fingers around the human's much smaller ones. "Are you into role play, too?"

In truth, Westram wouldn't have cared either way. Noah was his mate. He would happily take him any way he could get him.

Noah had yanked his hand away from Westram. "No," he stated flatly. With a scowl, he crossed his arms and curled his hands into fists. "I'm not. Nor do I care for one-night stands, flings, or getting my rocks off with any piece of ass who hits on me."

Westram opened his mouth, intending to apologize, but Noah turned away from him and addressed Arthur. "I hope this plan works fast," he stated. "I don't need some bruiser who only thinks with his dick dogging my steps."

"Westram does know how to be a gentleman," Alpha Kaiser claimed reassuringly.

When Noah scoffed and moved toward the table, perhaps

to retrieve one of the beers sitting on it, Kaiser turned his attention back to Westram and arched one brow in silent question.

Wincing for just an instant, Westram cut his gaze toward Noah, then refocused on his alpha.

Alpha Kaiser narrowed his eyes, but since neither Noah or Jacob knew about shifters — and they didn't plan to tell them unless absolutely necessary — not much could be said . . . yet.

"How are you doing?"

Westram didn't quite manage to hide his jerk of surprise upon hearing Beta William's softly spoken question, which yanked him out of his thoughts.

Meeting William's understanding gaze, Westram opened his mouth, then closed it again. He rubbed at his chest, his heart sending phantom pains through him at being separated from his mate. Instead of answering, Westram just shook his head.

William nodded. "Yeah, I sorta thought that when I saw the vacant glint in your eyes." Resting his hand on Westram's nape, he squeezed supportively. "Do you need a break to compose yourself?"

Bowing his head a little, Westram admitted, "I don't know if that will help." Grimacing, he told the beta, "My shark is pushing me to jump into the ocean so he can swim down to San Diego, and we can track Noah down." Upon seeing the concern enter William's green eyes, Westram quickly added, "I know that's not a possibility. My mate doesn't want to see me, and the only way I can swim these days is with you or Kaiser near me."

Having met Noah Redruvian months before, Westram's longnosed saw-shark was becoming damn pushy. His animal didn't understand the problem. He wanted Westram to grab the man, toss him into the ocean, and let the shark drag him home — literally.

So not an option.

Alpha Kaiser and his brother, William, were both huge squid—although not the same kind—and could keep his shark from taking off.

William nodded, squeezed his neck once more, then released him. "Well, take off anyway. Arthur wants to talk to you."

Confused, even as Westram nodded, he commented, "I thought he was in video conferences all day."

"He was supposed to be," William confirmed, shoving his hands into his pockets. "So it must be something important for him to step out for a few minutes and text me to get you."

Westram nodded. "I'll hurry over there." Then he started speed walking in the direction that would take him out of the north gate of the park. The narrow paved road led to a sprawling complex of condominiums. Most of the people working at the park lived there. Many were shifters with a smattering of human mates thrown in.

In Kaiser's suite, he'd set up a massive office for Arthur to work remotely from. The human owned an engineering business out of San Diego. On the occasions he couldn't do something from their location north of Sacramento, Kaiser would fly there with Arthur on a private jet.

Westram knew Noah worked as an accountant, so he would be able to work from anywhere, too. He had even already moved into a larger suite and fitted one of the rooms as an elaborate home office. Westram just had to figure out how to convince Noah that he was sincere.

Except, how can I do that when he won't even take my calls?

Arthur told Westram to be patient. He was putting a good word in for him, but it would take time. Evidently, his ex-boyfriend had been a cheating bastard who'd mentally abused Noah. The man needed time to heal before accepting the fact that Westram wasn't just like him.

Westram wished he could help Noah heal, but his beautiful mate wasn't ready to accept his advances, yet.

Someday.

That was the only promise he could make to his shark.

We have time. We're only a little over two hundred years old. We'll have centuries together, once Noah is ready.

Those were the thoughts Westram clung to when he lay down to sleep at night with loneliness causing his gut to clench and his arms aching to hold his human and soothe away all his fears.

Once Westram was out of the marine park, he broke into a sprint. He streaked up the path as fast as his legs would carry him. Being a shifter, that was pretty quickly, so it only took him a couple of minutes to reach Kaiser and Arthur's apartment.

Westram's knock on the door was immediately answered by Arthur. The human wore a headset, and he was speaking into it. At the same time, he beckoned Westram into the room.

"Yes, George," Arthur was saying. "I apologize, but I need that five-minute break now." A smile creased his lips as he chuckled softly. "I'm glad the restroom break is welcomed. I'm putting the call on hold, and I'll be back in five."

Then Arthur hit a button on the left side of the earpiece. He took the device off his head and set it on the coffee table. Turning away, he began to pace while scrubbing his fingers through his hair.

Seeing the alpha-mate's tension, Westram shifted uneasily. "If there's anything I can do to help . . ." he began, hoping the human would confide in him.

"I know, Westram," Arthur replied immediately, turning to face him. "I called you because it's about Noah."

Westram's gut clenched. "Noah?" Seeing the grimace on Arthur's face, he hated the bad feeling that burst through him. "What's wrong with Noah?"

Arthur shrugged, his expression appearing helpless. "I'm not sure. That's the problem."

The butterflies in his stomach morphed into bile in his

throat. "What do you mean?"

"He hasn't responded to my calls or texts in two days," Arthur told him. "That's never happened before. He's always prompt." Running his hands through his hair again, Arthur continued, "I'd go see him, but I have three days of meetings I just can't reschedule. I—"

"I'll go," Westram cut in. "Whether he wants to see me or not, I'll see what's going on."

Sighing with obvious relief, Arthur nodded. "I thought you'd say that. I have the jet being readied at the airport." After a second of hesitation, he added, "Maybe take Doc Keller and Solomon with you?"

Westram growled as his uneasiness turned to a feral need to see his mate safe and healthy. "You think there was trouble?"

Arthur shook his head. "I sure as hell hope not, but he made an odd comment the last time I spoke with him. Something about feeling as if he was being watched." Frowning, Arthur told him, "When I questioned him about it, Noah laughed it off and said he was just being paranoid. Then he changed the subject."

Turning toward the door, Westram claimed, "I'm on it."

No matter what, Westram would make certain his mate was safe, even if he had to endure some yelling from the man to do it.

Pain radiated through every inch of Noah. His body shivered, and he didn't know if it was caused by the chill of the bathroom tile floor beneath his naked frame or if it was due to his injuries. He felt as if his bruises had bruises.

Noah knew he had two broken fingers from when the man had first arrived and Noah had tried to call nine-one-one. After breaking his phone, the guy had tied him to a chair and snapped the pinky and ring finger on his right hand — one for each button he'd punched.

With tears threatening, through clenched teeth, Noah had asked, "Who are you? What do you want?"

Curling his lip, the man had claimed, "You know who I am." He narrowed his eyes as he added, "And I want you to suffer like I suffered."

Before Noah could deny knowing the man, the guy had slipped on a set of brass knuckles. He'd shut his mouth damn fast. Just in time, too, because the man had struck him across the jaw.

Noah had seen stars. He'd never been in a fight in his life, and he wasn't a big guy by any means. The tears fell then, but he'd managed to keep his mouth shut.

Well, that was until the man had heel-kicked him in the balls. His reflexive shout as a spike of agony coursed through his groin drew a derisive laugh from the stranger. Doubling over, Noah could do little but keep breathing through the pain.

The man didn't allow him but a moment to try to compose himself. Grabbing Noah's hair, he'd forced him to sit back up. The grin on his face caused a new spike of fear to go through him.

Deranged.

That was what the man looked like. There was just something in his pale blue eyes that told Noah the guy wasn't playing with a full deck.

"Don't worry, Noah," the man told him, revealing that even though Noah didn't recognize the guy, he obviously knew him. "By the time I'm done with you, you'll never need your balls again."

Then the man began pummeling his midsection. Each time Noah tried to double over and protect his soft areas, the stranger forced him back up. Finally, after one too many hits to the jaw, he'd blacked out.

Noah had woken naked and on the bathroom floor. For just an instant, he feared he'd been violated. A clench of his chute told him otherwise.

Still, being naked, Noah wondered if that was still on the stranger's agenda.

"Ah, you're awake. Good."

The man sauntered into the bathroom in a nicely pressed suit. His winning smile hid his crazy in a startling way.

If Noah had passed the man on the street, he never would have guessed at the psychopath hiding beneath the surface.

"Well, I must take off now, but I'll be back after work," the guy told him. Then his smile turned predatory. "So we can have some more fun."

He took a step closer, and Noah couldn't help but flinch, which caused the stranger to tip his head back and laugh.

Noah tried to slide along the floor away from the distracted man, but the movement caught his attention.

Continuing to smile widely, the guy stated, "Now, we can't have you trying to leave, now can we?" Then he pulled a baseball bat from behind the open door. Smacking it against his palm, he stared at Noah's legs. "Which one, which one?" he sing-songed.

Before Noah could even comprehend what the man intended, he struck, slamming the bat against his left knee. The scream had barely erupted from Noah's throat before blackness took him again.

Noah had woken later — he didn't know how long — to find his knee in a splint and his wrist handcuffed to the bathroom's radiator.

When the man had eventually returned, he hadn't beaten him. Instead, he'd pulled a razor blade from his pocket. While humming, he'd begun making shallow cuts in the flesh of Noah's arms, legs, and along his ribcage.

Delirious with pain, Noah had watched the guy use a towel to sop up the mess off the dark tile floor.

So that's why I'm in here.

The inane thought floated in and out of his mind before he once again welcomed oblivion.

CHAPTER TWO

Staring at the small house Noah lived in, Westram felt anticipation and dread surge through him in equal measure. He needed to know what was going on with his mate, but he feared Noah's response to him just showing up at his door. In the past, his mate hadn't been interested in listening to anything he had to say.

Gods, I hope that's changed.

"His car's in the driveway," Solomon commented, leaning forward from the back seat. "We gonna do this?" Then he winked, a smirk quirking up the corner of the big blond's lips. "Or sit here and pine for a while longer?"

Westram growled softly as he glared at the human. He worked security at *World of Aquatica*. As he was mated to Doctor Anthony Keller, there was no way the big man would have allowed his mate out of his sight, which was why Arthur recommended they both be asked.

"Leave him alone, Sol," Anthony chided softly. "He's been waiting on his mate to come around for months." The doc pinned Westram with an understanding look. "I don't know how you're managing to hold on, Wes."

"Thanks, Doc," Westram murmured. Then he opened his door and slipped from behind the wheel.

Solomon and Anthony followed his lead.

Westram strode up the walk, noticing the front curtain move in his peripheral vision. Hoping that his mate would open the door to him, he climbed the single patio step. After clenching and unclenching his fingers once, Westram rang the bell.

The wait felt like an eternity, even though it couldn't have been more than a minute.

No answer.

Solomon reached past Westram and rang the bell again, twice.

When that didn't elicit a response, Solomon knocked on the door and hollered, "We can do this all day, Noah. Open up."

Finally, the sound of the door locks disengaging reached Westram's ears. He held his breath. Except, the guy who opened it wasn't Noah.

The stranger was slender but toned, revealed by the navy-blue t-shirt and black jeans he wore. He stood just shy of six feet, and frowned at them with pale-blue eyes. While he glanced between them, the peppery scent of his unease filled Westram's nostrils.

"Geez," the man whispered. "Wake the whole neighborhood, why don't ya?"

"I want to see Noah," Westram stated bluntly. There was something about the man that made his shark uneasy. "I see his car here. Let us in."

Scoffing, the man shook his head. "Uh, no. I'm Noah's boyfriend, and he didn't mention any other friends coming." He frowned. "Besides, he wouldn't want anyone to see him while he's under the weather. Noah is private like that."

The acrid scent of lies perfumed the air.

Westram's shark roared in his mind, and he gritted his teeth, barely staying his desire to shove the door open and push past the lying human.

Which part is a lie? No way Arthur wouldn't have told me if Noah had started dating again.

"I'm calling bullshit," Westram snarled, stepping closer. "Open the door, and let us in."

The human narrowed his eyes, appearing as if he intended to refuse.

Anthony stepped forward, placing his hand on Westram's arm. "I'm Doctor Keller," he told the human. "If Noah is feeling under the weather, I'd like to check on him."

Obviously realizing that he couldn't send them away, the man sighed as he nodded. "Okay. I need to zip home to feed my cat, anyway." He opened the door wide as he grabbed his jacket from a nearby hook. As he slid his feet into a pair of sneakers by the door, he glanced at them and asked, "You mind keeping an eye on him until I get back?"

"Of course," Anthony replied.

Westram ignored him in favor of stepping inside the house and peering around. He'd stayed in Noah's home while guarding him. It had been the longest week of his life, since he hadn't been able to touch his prickly mate.

"Hey," Solomon called from behind him. "What's your name? So we can tell him where you went."

"Patrick," he claimed, the sound of his footsteps telling Westram that he was hustling down the sidewalk.

Westram ignored the exchange in favor of heading to Noah's bedroom. Even though he wanted to call out, he didn't. If Patrick was telling the truth and Noah was ill and sleeping, he didn't want to wake him.

But would it explain why Noah wasn't returning Arthur's calls?

Reaching Noah's bedroom, Westram carefully turned the knob. He eased the door open, praying the hinges didn't squeak. Frowning, he stared at the empty bed.

Where?

The sound of a whimper coming from the ensuite bathroom caught Westram's attention. Crossing to the closed door, he hesitated. Even though Westram knew he was probably the last person Noah would want to see, he girded up his courage and knocked softly on the door.

When Westram heard no response, he frowned. "Noah?" he called softly. Still nothing . . . not even yelling. "Noah, baby? You okay?"

Even his slip of the tongue, inserting an endearment, didn't get a response.

"How is he?" Anthony asked from the doorway.

Westram grimaced and shook his head. "Noah, talk to me or I'm coming in," he warned firmly.

When Noah still didn't reply, Westram took a deep breath, praying for courage. Then the scent of iron flitted across his nostrils. Shock coursed through Westram's system as did arousal.

For an instant, Westram didn't understand.

Then it hit him.

"I smell Noah's blood," Westram whispered.

Anthony rushed forward, ordering, "Open the door, Wes."

Westram didn't need to be told twice. The door wasn't locked, and he shoved it open. The sight before him caused a cry of dismay to erupt from his throat.

His sweet, beautiful mate lay sprawled on the bathroom floor, naked. His left wrist was handcuffed to the radiator, and dozens of shallow cuts marred his body. Two fingers of his right hand were obviously broken, and there was a crude brace on his left knee. Beneath the cuts were so many colorful bruises, he could barely see any unmarred flesh.

"Noah," Westram cried, his voice breaking as he rushed forward.

"Oh, fuck," Solomon whispered.

Westram hit his knees even as he turned and glared at the other man. Except, Solomon was already pivoting. Then the human sprinted from the room.

Turning his attention back to Noah, Westram hovered his hands over him. He didn't know where it was safe to touch. There seemed to be marks damn near everywhere.

"Remove the handcuff first," Anthony ordered from where he knelt on one knee beside him. "Then I'm going to need to run my hands over his torso to check for rib or spinal damage.

Can you handle me touching your naked mate?"

As Westram nodded, he willed his roaring shark to calm. The doc would fix his mate. He had to.

Gently lifting Noah's wrist, Westram placed it in his lap. He carefully gripped the metal. With a quick wrench, he broke the offending item.

"You're safe now, my mate," Westram whispered, leaning close to the man who already held his heart. Vowing it to be true, he stated, "I'll never let anyone hurt you again."

Quiet murmuring broke into Noah's consciousness. He bit the inside of his cheek, forcing back his desire to cry out as pain blanketed his senses once more. If the psycho knew he'd woken, he knew he would have to withstand another round of some new torture.

Gods, why is this happening to me? Who is he? Why hasn't someone come looking for me? Hasn't it been long enough?

Noah had thought one of his buddies would have come looking for him . . . if he just held out long enough.

"Easy, Noah," a voice crooned into his ear. "You're safe now. You can open your eyes."

Upon hearing the deep voice Noah had been trying to banish from his mind for months, he tensed. That caused a spike of agony to flare through his torso and out to his limbs. Unable to help himself, a cry of pain burst past his lips.

As Noah inhaled and exhaled, trying to gain control of himself, the expected maniacal laughter never came. Instead, he felt the gentle, soothing touch of someone stroking ever-so-lightly over his torso, then down his arms, before sliding back up to thread through his hair to massage his scalp.

Peeling his eyelids open, Noah blinked a few times, trying to clear his blurry vision.

"Take it slow, my mate," Westram's unmistakable voice purred into Noah's ear. "You are safe." The press of lips to his temple registered before Westram murmured, "I'll never allow Patrick near you again."

Unable to help himself, while still struggling to focus, Noah rasped, "Who's Patrick?"

Noah thought his words sounded horribly slurred, but Westram seemed to have understood him, for he told him, "There was a man here when we arrived." Westram continued to massage Noah's scalp, then lowered his hand and teased over his collarbone. "He said you were sick. Claimed to be your boyfriend." That last word Westram said on a growl. "Knew he was lying."

Breathing slow and deep hurt, but Noah did it anyway. He finally managed to get his bleary eyes to focus ... well, as much as he could without his glasses. Without turning his head, he took in the familiar surroundings.

"I'm in my bedroom," Noah mumbled, more to himself than to Westram. "And you're here." That was when something else registered. "In my bed. Naked." Scowling, Noah gathered the fortitude to turn his head and scowl at the man lying behind him, holding him, his hot bare flesh pressed against Noah's own. "Did you take liberties while I'm injured?"

As soon as the words left his mouth, Noah felt like a complete and utter ass. He saw Westram jerk beside him. A look of devastation crossed his features.

"No," Westram whispered, even as he began to ever-so-carefully disentangle their limbs ... and they *were* tangled. He had one leg between Noah's own. His left arm lay under Noah's pillow, and his body was flush to Noah's. "I'd never do that."

"Stop," Noah whispered, gripping the arm Westram was pulling from around his waist. "Please. I didn't mean it. I—" Tears burned the edges of his eyes. "I—" Noah just didn't know how to finish that.

I'm an asshole would have fit.

Westram immediately relaxed against him again. "It's okay, Noah," he murmured, his voice sounding resigned. "I know I'm the last person you want to see."

"That's not true," Noah blurted out, then instantly wondered if he was on some kind of heavy pain meds. Considering the way the fingers on his right hand were wrapped and how he could feel a much bulkier brace on his left knee, he figured he must have received some kind of medical attention.

"It's not?" Westram sounded so damn hopeful.

Noah hesitated for an instant, but when he saw the guarded look begin to descend over Westram's features, he whispered, "It's not. I've always been attracted to you, but" — he hesitated but knew he needed to go with the truth — "I'm not the party or club or one-night stand type. I can't accept just one night from a guy anymore, so it'd be easier if we didn't even start."

To Noah's shock, Westram grinned widely at him. "Oh, Noah." He huffed a soft sigh as he shook his head once, twice. Then his deep gray eyes filled with a heated glow that took Noah's breath away. "Noah, my mate." Westram spoke slowly, emphasizing each word. "You are it for me."

Opening his mouth to reply — how, Noah wasn't certain after that shocking declaration — but Westram touched his fingertips to his upper lip.

"I know you don't believe me, Noah," Westram murmured, a kind smile curving his lips. "And that's okay, because we don't really know each other." Then Westram smiled roguishly as he winked. "But now that you've given me the go-ahead, that will change because you're it for me, Noah."

Noah stared in shock.

Did that really just happen?

Perhaps Noah was still unconscious or dreaming on the

floor of his bathroom. He could be hallucinating from pain. Maybe he was out of his head because he didn't want to wake up still cuffed to his bathroom's radiator.

"This *is* happening, my mate," Westram told him, perhaps reading his expression. "I'm yours, and you're mine." Leaning close, he pecked a kiss to the corner of Noah's mouth before drawing back and whispering, "I'll give you the time you need to accept it."

Not knowing what else to do, Noah just nodded.

Westram eyed him through a narrowed gaze for a few seconds, then eased back onto the bed. Sighing deeply, he cuddled up close behind Noah. His body's heat poured through Noah's backside, warming him in a surprisingly soothing manner.

"So," Westram murmured, his warm breath fanning over Noah's ear. "It seems we'll both have some questions for each other." Rubbing up and down Noah's upper arm, Westram murmured, "Let's start with why I'm in bed with you. I'll set your mind at ease."

Relaxing against the pillow, Noah nodded once. Then he grimaced because the move hurt his jaw.

"Damn, how about some pain meds?" Westram muttered once again rising onto his arm. "Doc told me you can have a couple of these once you wake."

Noah turned his head a little so he could watch Westram reach behind himself. He picked up something off the nightstand and held them in his flattened palm, showing him two oval, pale-blue pills.

"What are they?" Noah couldn't help but ask. He wasn't a big fan of drugs.

"Uhhh . . ." Westram's brows furrowed, and his cheeks took on a pinkish hue. "I'm embarrassed to say that I'm not totally certain." When Noah grimaced, Westram winked and said, "Just a sec. I'll find out." Without even raising his voice, only turning his head a little, Westram stated, "Doc, we need you in here."

Hearing the immediate response of the creak of furniture, then the soft thud of footsteps over his floorboards, Noah wondered how many people were aware of what had happened to him.

"Did you all call the cops?" Noah asked curiously. "Do I need to give a statement? Because I don't actually know who the bastard is who did this."

"Really?" Westram sounded a little surprised. "He introduced himself as Patrick, but I couldn't say if that was true or not. Too far away from him."

Noah didn't know what distance had to do with anything, but he shook his head. "I asked him who he was, but he only said I already knew, which I didn't." Frowning, remembering that first day, Noah added, "And he said he wanted to make me suffer the way he suffered."

Westram appeared troubled even as he hummed. "It does sound personal," he mumbled. "I wonder —"

Whatever Westram wondered would have to wait, since the bedroom door opened to reveal a broad-shouldered, auburn-haired man with warm blue-gray eyes. "Hey, Noah," he greeted, moving toward the bed slowly. "It's good to see you awake." His expression appeared kind as he added, "And not dripping with fever."

"Fever?" Noah glanced between the pair.

Nodding, Westram set the pills on the mattress near his head, then skimmed his fingertips along his collarbone. "That's the answer to your other question," he admitted. "I never would have taken such liberties without your permission if it weren't life and death." Westram's gaze flitted down Noah's blanket-covered body, an appreciative light filling his eyes for a second before he hid it. "As much as I love where I am, pressed against your gorgeous body, I never would have done it without invitation if I didn't need to bring your fever down."

The guy who had to be the doc nodded as he stopped beside the bed. "If your fever hadn't broken yesterday morning, I would have been forced to take you to the hospital." Grimacing, he added, "And it would have made it tough to keep the police out of this if we'd had to do that."

Confused even further, Noah asked, "You didn't call the police?"

Westram shook his head. "When it comes to matters that pertain to mates, we handle things in-house."

Noah felt his head begin to swim—or maybe it had been creeping up on him for a while—but he began struggling to focus. Sleep threatened to take him back under. Swallowing hard, he blinked a few times.

"In-house?"

What did that mean?

"We have so much to explain," Westram told him. Then he asked, "Anthony, what are the pills you gave to me to give Noah? He's not a fan of drugs."

"Oh." The doc—Anthony—smiled at Noah. Then he rattled off something that Noah didn't think he could re-pronounce, which caused the doc to grin wider. "Sorry. It's just a strong naproxen. It'll take the edge off your broken fingers, cracked ribs, sprained knee, and the plethora of bruises you have until you can bond with Westram." Anthony winked. "Then it won't be long before your enhanced healing kicks in and you won't need them anymore."

Enhanced healing? Bonding?

Uncertain what else to say, Noah went with, "Oh," before picking up the pills and popping them into his mouth. "Thank you," he mumbled, accepting the straw Westram offered.

Then Noah relaxed back onto the bed and let sleep take him.

If this was a dream, he didn't know how his battered mind

could have come up with it.

CHAPTER THREE

Westram lifted his gaze to Anthony's after he'd placed the cup back on the nightstand. "I hadn't told him about that, yet."

Anthony opened his mouth, then closed it again. "Oh." Crossing his arms over his chest, he cocked his head. "Soooo . . . Arthur told Noah nothing of our kind? Or way of life?"

After shaking his head, Westram cuddled back up to Noah's back, tucking the blanket more tightly around him. "No. He didn't want to share any of that until he accepted my attention," he explained, keeping his voice barely above a whisper. Smiling at Anthony, Westram murmured, "That time is now. Don't worry."

"I'll be back in a couple of hours to check his bandages unless you call for me earlier."

Westram smiled at the doc, then relaxed with his mate. He tucked his nose against his sweet-smelling mate's hair and breathed in his scent. For the first time in months, he finally felt settled.

The only way it could have been better was if Noah hadn't been injured.

But he'll get better.

With those thoughts filling his mind, Westram allowed his body to doze.

Westram roused to the sound of whimpers. Snapping open

his eyelids, he stared at Noah. His sweet mate moved restlessly against him, and soft sounds of distress escaped his lips.

With his mate clearly in the throes of some nightmare, Westram began rubbing his arm, hoping to soothe. "You're okay, Noah," he murmured into his mate's ear as he nuzzled his cheek against the side of his human's head. "Come back to me, my love. You're still safe, right here in my arms. I'll always keep you safe."

For an instant, Noah stiffened, and Westram feared his touch wouldn't work. Then, to his relief, his mate sighed deeply. His body relaxed, and he pressed closer to Westram's body, perhaps seeking his warmth or comfort.

Either way, Westram let out his own sigh of relief. His mate was accepting, even seeking out, his touch. He continued to gently glide his fingers over Noah's arm, then up to his shoulder before rubbing down his chest. Having waited so long to hold his mate, to touch him, Westram thrilled in the simple activity of just being with him.

A change in Noah's breathing told Westram that his mate had woken. He didn't change his ministrations. Instead, he waited to see what Noah would do or say.

Something in Westram told him everything hinged on the next few minutes.

"You stayed," Noah whispered.

Westram didn't know why that surprised Noah, but he could scent his human's shock. "Of course, I stayed," he murmured, enjoying the quiet of the moment.

"I was horrible to you," Noah stated.

"No, you weren't," Westram countered, pressing his nose against Noah's nape. "You were protecting yourself and healing from an asshole's assholishness."

To Westram's pleasure, Noah snickered. "I don't think that's a word."

Westram lifted one shoulder in a half-shrug as he smiled

against the warm flesh under his lips. "Eh." Then he licked Noah's skin just to enjoy his mate's flavor.

"Did you just lick me?"

Realizing how that could confuse his human mate, Westram eased his head away just a little. "I did," he admitted. "You taste exquisite."

Noah began shifting, so Westram eased his hold, eager to see what his mate needed. To his pleasure, his mate only turned to lie on his back. He peered up at him with confusion filling his gorgeous green eyes, squinting a little.

"I found your glasses," Westram told him. Grimacing, he added, "One arm was broken. Solomon took them to an eye place and they put the lenses into similar frames, but they're not totally the same." He reached behind him and grabbed them off the nightstand, then held them out to Noah. "I hope they're okay. We can change them again when you feel up to rising."

"Why didn't you call the cops?" Noah asked, taking the glasses and sliding them on his face. His half-swollen closed left eye remained squinting, but his right stared at Westram steadily. Noah's expression appeared troubled. "That psycho needs to be caught."

"And we *will* catch him, Noah," Westram assured. Then he sighed. Unable to stop touching without his mate expressly telling him to, and needing the connection for what he prepared to say next, Westram rested his palm on Noah's bare torso. "You remember when Anthony made a comment about bonding and increased healing? Before you fell asleep earlier?"

Noah slipped his tongue out and ran it over his bottom lip.

The move drew Westram's attention, and he barely held in a moan. He wanted to trace that path with his own tongue so damn badly.

Then Westram pulled his head out of his ass and asked,

"Do you need some more water?"

"Actually," Noah whispered, his gaze straying to the en-suite door. "I really need to piss, but I—" He swallowed so hard his Adam's apple bobbed.

When Noah finished his thought, it nearly tore Westram's heart from his chest.

"I never want to go back into that room again."

Westram understood completely. That was probably where much of Noah's abuse had been done. He nodded and began to rise, pushing the comforter and sheet from their bodies.

"Then I'll take you to the other bathroom," Westram declared. He quickly grabbed a pair of loose sleep pants Solomon had purchased for them both while running other errands. "Move slowly," he ordered as he pulled his own on before helping his mate ease to the side of the bed. "You have a lot of injuries."

Noah nodded, his jaw flexing as Westram helped him into his own pair of pants, doing his best not to stare at his mate's beautiful body. Then he wrapped his arm around Noah's waist and helped him to his feet. Carefully, he began guiding his limping human out of the bedroom. While Westram would have much rather just picked Noah up and carried him, he didn't think his mate would appreciate that without permission.

Maybe another time.

Westram liked the idea of holding Noah in his arms . . . for any reason.

Guiding Noah into the bathroom, Westram asked, "Do you need help?"

Noah rested his weight against the vanity while shaking his head. "No, thank you." Wrapping his arms around his waist, perhaps trying to hide his lean, bruise-covered torso — which was already half-covered by bandages from Anthony cleaning up the human's cuts — Noah told him, "I can do this alone."

Even though Westram understood Noah's desire for privacy while taking care of his bodily needs, he couldn't believe the amount of self-control it took for him to nod and walk away from his injured mate.

"I'll be right outside if you need me," Westram told Noah, exiting the room. As he closed the door, he stated softly, "Just call."

Standing in the hallway, Westram scrubbed his hand through his dark-gray hair before pushing it behind his ear. He noticed movement to his left and saw Anthony moving toward him.

"Everything okay?" the other shifter asked quietly, obviously doing his best to keep their conversation private from Noah on the other side of the door.

Westram nodded once. "He asked why we didn't call the cops, so I'm about to share shifters with him." Grimacing, he muttered, "How did Solomon take it?"

Anthony chuckled softly as he smirked. "He didn't believe me. I had to prove it."

"Not easy when we turn into sharks and we don't have the grotto around," Westram pointed out, referring to a massive underground lake located underneath their condominium complex.

"We'll figure it out," Anthony assured, patting him on the shoulder.

Hearing the toilet flush, Westram cocked his head and listened. He heard Noah's shuffling steps, then the sound of the faucet running. When it shut off, Anthony gave him another reassuring smile and headed back to the living room.

A second later, the door opened, and Westram peered into the pale, pinched face of his injured human.

Unable to help himself, Westram bent and lifted Noah into his arms. His mate squeaked and flailed for an instant. Once

Westram got him settled against his chest, Noah stilled.

"I could walk," Noah claimed as Westram started back toward the bedroom.

"I know." Westram winked. "But I sure like this better."

Noah's cheeks pinked, and he opened his mouth. Then his stomach growled, interrupting him.

Westram paused in the doorway to the bedroom and met Noah's gaze. "You've been asleep for the last two days," he told Noah. "I bet you're starving."

Why didn't I think of that before?

Nodding, Noah bit his bottom lip. "I don't remember the last time I ate," he admitted. "That asshole tossed me a couple of rolls one of the days, but I don't know when that was." Noah frowned as he suddenly asked, "What day is it?"

"Wednesday the seventeenth," Westram answered honestly.

The blood drained from Noah's face, leaving his already pale features a pasty color. "Shit," he whispered. "Six days."

"I can't believe I lost so much time," Noah muttered.

"That you survived three days with him proves your strength and resilience," Westram told him, his voice gruff. "I'm sorry it took us so long to get to you."

"Did Arthur send you?" Noah asked, figuring that was the only reason Westram would have come.

Westram nodded as he started moving forward again. "He said you weren't answering texts or calls, and he couldn't get away." Pausing beside the bed, his expression serious, Westram told him, "And if I'd known you were in trouble, I would have come without his prompting."

"But I blocked your number," Noah reminded him. "Why are you being so nice?" When Westram began placing him back on the bed, Noah squeezed his forearm. "Wait. Can we sit in the living room?" Something in the man's deep gray eyes told him they were about to have a serious conversation. "And get food, too?"

"Absolutely." Westram immediately acquiesced, turning around to head back out of the room. "What would you like to eat?" Before Noah could answer, Westram continued, "Maybe we should talk to the doc to see what you can have."

"Is Anthony really a doctor?" Noah asked, disbelieving. "I don't know any doctors that make house calls these days."

Westram grinned. "Yeah, Anthony's a doctor. He works with us at *World of Aquatica*," he told him. "You'll meet Solomon, too. He's the doc's mate."

While Noah's memories were a little fuzzy, he recalled something. "Isn't that what you called me? Mate?"

Nodding, Westram told him, "And I'll explain." He sighed as he entered the living room. "I have so much to explain." Then he settled Noah onto the corner of the sofa and grabbed the throw blanket from off the back. "Here. Let's get you comfortable."

Noah accepted the attention, surprised at how caring Westram was, especially after the way he'd rebuffed him. He'd never had a boyfriend care for him when he was sick, but it sure felt nice when Westram did it. In truth, Noah knew he could get used to it super fast.

Maybe I should have given him a chance months ago. If I had, would he have been around to stop that asshole?

"Hey, you okay?" Westram asked, crouching beside him and rubbing his fingertips over the back of one of his hands. "You're safe now, my love. You'll heal," he continued. "We'll figure out who this guy is and stop him."

"But I don't even know who he is," Noah murmured, frowning at Westram. "How?"

"Well, we know two things about him," Solomon stated, leaning forward from where he'd been sitting in a nearby recliner. He held out his hand. "I'm Solomon Lynch, by the way. Anthony's partner."

Noah reached out and took the big man's hand, taking in his close-cropped military cut and broad, strong frame. "Nice to meet you." After releasing the man's hand, he blurted out, "You're gay?"

Solomon chuckled as he settled back in his chair. "As the day is long." Then he winked and returned him to their discussion. "So, we know that the man's name is Patrick and that he has a cat."

"You sure?" Westram asked as he rose and headed toward the kitchen. "What can Noah have to eat, Doc?" he asked the man who was moving around Noah's kitchen as if he owned the space. "He's not certain when he ate last."

"I'm going to start him on chicken noodle soup and buttered bread," Anthony told him. Smiling at Noah, the doc winked. "Just like Momma used to make."

Noah scoffed softly, but he returned the man's smile. "My mom couldn't cook anything that didn't come out of a can or frozen box," he admitted. Thoughts of his mother caused his smile to slip. "And I haven't talked to her since I came out at nineteen."

Solomon hummed. "One of *those* mothers, huh?" He shook his head. "I'm sorry, man."

"Family is what we make it to be," Anthony stated, passing a bowl over the counter to Westram. "You have a coffee maker and grounds, so I'm assuming you drink it. Do you want a cup?"

Noah shook his head as his stomach turned just at the thought. "Actually, I don't," he admitted, taking the bowl of soup from Westram. "I keep it around for others. Jacob picked out the coffee brand last time, so hope you all like it."

"It's okay," Solomon told him, clearly a blunt man. He grinned. "But I was in the military, and I'm used to drinkin' swill, too, so my opinion may not be the best one to go by."

Chuckling softly, Noah rested the bowl on his lap, then

took the spoon Westram was holding out. "Thanks," he murmured to the attentive man.

"What would you like to drink, then?" Westram asked, touching his fingertips to Noah's jaw tenderly, skimming around his bruises. "And drink slowly. I bet your jaw is still aching."

"Orange juice, if there is any," Noah murmured, mesmerized by the look of affection in Westram's gray eyes. "Never had a guy look at me like you do." Feeling his cheeks heat, Noah knew he blushed. "Didn't mean to say that out loud."

Westram grinned, his eyes darkening with obvious pleasure. "I'll look at you like this every day of our lives if you let me," he whispered before bending and pressing a kiss to his temple. "I see Anthony found the juice. Be right back."

Forcing himself to *not* stare at Westram's sleep-pants-covered ass, Noah focused on the soup and took a bite. He hummed appreciatively as the smooth, rich flavor burst across his taste buds. Scooping up more, he quickly took another bite.

CHAPTER FOUR

Westram watched Noah eat the soup with a hearty appetite. His mate dipped the buttered bread into the broth before taking a bite and hummed appreciatively as he chewed. Even the orange juice made Noah sigh just loud enough for Westram to hear it from where he sat eating beside him on the sofa.

While Westram agreed the food and drink was good, Noah's obvious enjoyment of it told him his mate had been starved.

So who the fuck is the asshole?

Waiting to bring it up until Noah finished eating was damn difficult, but Westram wanted his mate's meal to be in a comfortable environment. Fortunately, the others must have picked up on that, for they didn't speak of anything other than the food while they ate. Anthony shared how his mother had taught him how to cook, since she hadn't had any daughters.

Once the dishes had been set aside and refills of coffee and orange juice had been made, Westram made himself comfortable with one arm around Noah's shoulders and his mate tucked against his side.

"Sooooo," Solomon mused before blowing on his fresh cup of coffee. "You asked how we confirmed the guy's name was Patrick?" He peered pointedly at Anthony. "My man was close enough to scent that he told the truth, even if you weren't."

Westram took that at face value and nodded.

Noah didn't. "*Scented* the truth?"

Blowing out a breath, Westram nodded slowly. "We'll explain that in a minute," he promised before turning his attention back to Solomon. "And the cat thing was true, too?"

Solomon winked as he grinned widely. "And I watched him long enough to see him get into his two-thousand-twelve or thirteen *Toyota Prius*." Relaxing back in his chair, he added, "Plus, I noticed his license plate number. I've sent it all, along with a crude sketch, to Ovram."

Gaping at Solomon, Westram stared at the doc's human. Ovram was their pod's tech guru. Armed with that information, he should easily be able to track down the psycho who'd harmed his mate.

"Why didn't you tell me?"

"*I* made the decision," Anthony told him. "I wanted you focused on your mate instead of going off half-cocked to track the bastard down." He pointed at Noah. "He needed you."

Westram nodded slowly. "I understand," he murmured, turning his attention on Noah. Rubbing his fingertips over his mate's cheek, he traced along the edge of the bruise marring his jaw. "They're right. I would have wanted to track the bastard down."

"So, we know who he is?" Noah whispered, his brows creasing. "Has he been caught?"

Solomon shook his head. "Not caught, yet, but he will be." His eyes narrowed as a cold gleam entered his blue eyes. "Dare and Pisces are already in the city. As soon as Ovram confirms a location, they'll be dispatched to track him down." He pointed between himself and Anthony as he waggled his eyebrows. "We're here to give you two a safe environment to bond."

"Bond," Noah whispered. "There's that word again."

"And now for the crazy explanation," Solomon said, turning serious again. "You're probably not going to believe us until we show you proof, but your bathtub isn't big enough for that."

Noah cocked his head. "Bathtub? Proof?" He glanced around at everyone, his shoulders tensing. "What's going on?"

"If Arthur were here, he'd corroborate everything," Westram began slowly. "But he's not." Then a thought struck. "Do you think he's off his conference calls, yet?"

Anthony shrugged. "Only one way to check." He pulled out his cell phone and dialed, then put it on speaker and set it on the coffee table.

"Hey, Doc." Arthur's voice came through the line. "How's Noah?"

"Noah is awake and sitting with us," Anthony replied, leaning forward to rest his forearms on his knees. "We're about to start the crazy explanations, and thought maybe you could help us convince him without having to take him out to sea."

Westram felt Noah tense even further beside him, and he realized how that had to have sounded to him. "I'll never allow anything to happen to you, Noah," he reminded the man he hoped to soon make his lover. "When we explain, you'll understand why Anthony phrased it that way."

Arthur's chuckle came through the line. "Not the best thing to say, Doc, but don't worry, Noah. You're totally safe with these guys." Then he cleared his throat before adding, "And what they're about to tell you may sound fantastic, but it's all true."

Noah glanced around at everyone. "Okay. Just spit it out, guys." He frowned as he used a finger to push his glasses up his nose. "What aren't you saying?"

Clearing his throat, Anthony arched one brow and stared pointedly at Westram.

Westram sighed and nodded. "Okay. See. Here's the

thing." Never would he have thought it so difficult to get the words out, but they needed to be said. "Humans aren't alone on this planet." Seeing Noah's eyes narrow, Westram quickly added, "Since the beginning of time, what are called paranormals have lived right alongside you. We keep ourselves secret, due to prejudice and persecution."

"Humans as a race don't exactly have a good track record for accepting people different than themselves," Arthur cut in helpfully. "Whether they believe a different religion, have a different skin color, body shape, sex, or sexuality. Humans have persecuted everyone different in some capacity, and some are still being persecuted. That's why paranormals keep themselves separate."

Licking his lips, Noah asked, "Okay. So what *is* a paranormal?"

After exchanging a quick look with the others, Westram stated, "There are many kinds, but Anthony and I are called shifters. We share our spirit, our mind, and our body, with an animal, and we can turn into it at will."

Predictably, Noah scoffed. "Yeah, right." He grinned. "Prove it."

Westram groaned, and he wasn't the only one.

Noah couldn't help but snicker as he heard the sounds of frustration escaping everyone.

But really. What did they expect? That I should just believe something so outlandish?

"Table the need for proof for a few minutes," Arthur told him through the phone. "Let them finish all the other things they need to share. Okay?"

Frowning in the direction of the phone, Noah stated, "You and I have known each other since we were teenagers. Hell, we lived together in college." After his mother had cut off support when he'd come out in college, he'd surfed his buddy's couch for months since he'd no longer been able to afford his apartment's rent. "Don't tell me you're suddenly claiming to be a paranormal shifter, too."

"Noooo," Arthur replied, drawing out the word. "I'm human. Same as you." After a second, he added, "Same as Solomon. But Westram and Anthony really are shifters."

Noah cocked his head even as his brows shot up. "How can you believe that?" His friend had always been so down to earth. "Did you get hit on the head or something?"

Arthur's low chuckle came through the line. "Naw. Not hit on the head. Just something I've seen with my own eyes. My lover, Kaiser, is their alpha, the leader. His brother, William, is called the beta, or second-in-command."

"Wait a minute." Noah lifted a hand, although he knew Arthur couldn't see it. "Alpha? Beta? Like in a wolf pack?"

"Sure," Arthur confirmed. "They're just not wolves. They're a myriad of aquatic and semi-aquatic shifters."

Noah rubbed his hand over the bridge of his nose underneath his glasses. "I—" He felt Westram take his hand, threading their fingers together. For some reason the gentle squeeze, coupled with the contact, sent soothing warmth through his body, helping him relax. Turning his attention to the man, Noah mumbled, "I don't see how it's possible for a human to change into a fish or vise-versa. It's just not anatomically possible."

"I wish I could show you right this instant to prove it to you," Westram told him with an understanding smile. "And no, it doesn't take the full moon. I just can't do it because I must be in water . . . and my saw-shark is a lot bigger than your bathtub."

"Saw-shark?"

Westram nodded. "Longnosed saw-shark with gills and fins and everything."

"But—" Noah stared into Westram's eyes, and he saw the

sincerity there. The man truly believed he changed into a . . . shark. "Why are you telling me this?" He glanced around at the others before refocusing on Westram. "If it's truly a secret, why tell me?"

"The only time a paranormal purposefully tells a human is when that human is their mate," Westram told him, holding his gaze, his expression appearing earnest. "The other half of our soul. The one person in all the world who can complete us, bond with us, and live our centuries-long life with us."

Noah's mind began to reel at that revelation, but Westram wasn't done.

Westram squeezed Noah's hand as he claimed, "That person is you, Noah. *You* are the other half of my soul. You're my everything." He brought Noah's hand to his lips. "Fate has brought us together, and I've been eagerly waiting for the chance to show you how much I can care for you."

Swallowing hard, Noah tried to take in all that Westram had expressed.

Fate. Mates. The bonding of souls.

Noah peered into Westram's gaze, took in his earnest expression, and could see so very clearly how badly the man wanted him to believe him.

Except, that would also mean —

"So, the only reason you're telling me all this is because Fate decided I'm your soul mate?" Lifting his hand, Noah added, "Not that I'm saying I believe all this, but" — he shrugged — "if it weren't for your idea of Fate, you wouldn't even care about me."

"Aaaand, that's my cue," Solomon drawled with a smile. He leaned over and gripped Anthony's hand. "Think of it this way." Using his free hand, Solomon waved between Noah and Westram. "You're standing in the middle of a crowded room. Lots of hot guys around, and across the way, you spot Westram. Your gazes meet, but there are so many people in the room, it'd be a pain in the ass to get over there." Solomon winked as his smile turned roguish. "All Fate does is give you that extra push to make the effort to cross that room." Snapping his fingers, Solomon added, "Oh, and sex is phenomenal between mates. Plus, there's no chance of your guy ever straying. Complete fidelity."

Gaping, Noah snapped his gaze to Westram. "Really?"

Westram nodded, his expression serious as he peered at Noah intently. "Yes, my mate," he replied in a soft tone. "You're it for me."

"And his shark has been pining for you and driving the rest of the guys at the park crazy," Anthony cut in, his tone a mixture of exasperation and sadness. "Accept him, his love, and let him dote on you for the rest of your lives."

Noah felt his body flush hot as the idea of being taken care of and what it entailed flashed through his mind. He couldn't count the number of dreams he'd had over the last several months of Westram's hands on him. Then morning would come, and he would be in bed alone, aching and needing.

That would never happen again.

Still, how could any of this be true?

"I don't know how to believe you," Noah admitted quietly, casting a beseeching look at Westram. "I mean, shifters? Paranormals? Really?"

Westram's mouth opened, then closed, his expression turning pained even as he nodded. "Proof," he whispered. "I get it."

"Too bad neither of us have the ability to partial shift like Alpha Kaiser and Beta William do," Anthony commented, drawing attention. "We *could* fly you to the marine park. Take you to the grotto, so you can see for yourself."

"If you're willing," Westram urged. "Will you come home with me? Arthur is there. He can reassure you, and I can prove that I'm telling the truth."

Noah thought about that.

Did he have enough faith in Westram and these others to

pick up and leave with them? Would they have come without Arthur's insistence?

Except, they could have just left him to be murdered by Patrick.

Sweeping his focus over Westram's face, Noah knew that if the man had somehow known he was in trouble, he would have come, no questions asked. The man truly believed everything they had told him.

Only one way to find out.

Besides, being with Westram and Arthur would be far safer until Patrick was found and put behind bars.

Just as Noah opened his mouth to agree, another thought struck him. "Wait," Noah murmured, cocking his head. "You never did say why you didn't call the cops."

"Oh. That's easy," Solomon answered, a dark smile curving his lips. "When a mate is threatened, if the human authorities aren't already involved, we take care of it on our own."

"On your . . ." Noah let his words fade off. "As in—" He wasn't certain how to finish that.

Westram squeezed his hand as he cupped Noah's jaw and urged him to meet his gaze. "Yes," he stated calmly. "That bastard threatened the mate of a shifter, whether he knew it or not. His life is forfeit."

"But if he walked away—" Noah began.

Anthony shrugged. "We could have a vampire alter his mind so he doesn't remember you and whatever happened to set him on this path." His lips twisted in a grimace as he added, "But how do we know something else wouldn't set him off and he wouldn't try to do something like this to someone else? That would be on our heads."

"I guess—" Noah gasped. "Vampire?"

Westram tugged Noah tighter against his side as he gave him a warm smile. "Welcome to the rabbit hole, Alice."

CHAPTER FIVE

A fter all this time, Westram could hardly believe it. He had his mate in his home . . . finally. While he knew Noah still didn't believe them about everything, that was okay.

He will . . . very soon. Then maybe he won't mind if I join him in my bed.

Westram had seen Noah's discomfort on the flight. Even a private jet was only so comfortable to the injured.

When they'd arrived at the Sacramento airport, Alpha Kaiser had a limo waiting for them. Noah had instantly fallen asleep in Westram's arms where they'd cuddled in the back seat. Upon arriving home, Westram had carried Noah upstairs and tucked him into his bed.

Anthony had given Noah a quick once-over, then proclaimed him tired and healing.

Safe in their own lands, Anthony and Solomon had headed to their own apartment.

Westram popped a cap on a beer, but he hadn't even reached the sofa when a quiet knock sounded on his door. Opening it, he wasn't surprised to see Alpha Kaiser and Arthur there. He swung the door wide, silently beckoning them to enter.

"How's he doing?" Alpha Kaiser asked softly while discreetly sniffing at Westram while he passed him. "You smell more settled, so something good has come of this."

Although Westram had thought the same thing a time or two, he still grimaced. "I hate that we've started coming together this way," he murmured. "And Doc says he's healing.

He's resting right now." When Kaiser nodded, Westram held up his beer. "Want one?"

"Sure," Kaiser confirmed. "Have any wine for Arthur?"

Arthur snorted. "You know, I don't mind drinking the occasional beer," he told him. Then with a wink, he added, "And water is a perfectly acceptable drink, too."

Kaiser pinned a look of warmth on Arthur reserved only for his mate. "And, yet, what does it hurt to ask if someone has your preference on hand?"

Gripping Kaiser's hand, Arthur murmured, "Of course."

"I do have wine, actually," Westram told them, heading back to his kitchen. "I bought a couple of bottles a while back because you told me Noah prefers it."

"You bought me wine even when I wasn't taking your calls?"

Hearing Noah's soft voice, Westram turned and peered toward the hallway. He spotted his mate leaning against the wall. While he appeared a little pale, Westram had never seen a better sight than his mate in his home.

Hurrying toward Noah, Westram nodded. "I had faith that Fate would bring us together eventually," he told him as he slipped his arm around Noah's waist and encouraged him to lean against him. "Are you ready for supper? It's just a take-and-bake pizza from *Papa Murphy's*, but I heard the barbeque chicken is your favorite?" With a wink, Westram added, "Arthur told me that, too."

Noah stared up at him in surprise even as he nodded a little. "It is." Cocking his head, he asked curiously, "Have you had it in your freezer a while, too?"

Westram shook his head. "Naw. I asked around and found out my friend Colton was out surfing with his mate. He picked it up for me and dropped it off in my fridge earlier today."

"That was so very thoughtful of you," Noah murmured,

allowing Westram to help him into one of the chairs at the oval dining room table. "You've went through a lot of trouble to find out about my likes and dislikes."

Westram shrugged. "You're my mate, Noah." He knew Noah wasn't completely on board with the whole *mate thing*, yet, but that hadn't stopped Westram from doing what he could to be prepared for when he would be. "I waited for you for almost two hundred years. While being separated for several months hurt, I would have waited longer until you accepted me."

As Westram spoke, he reached up and slid two wine glasses off the rack hanging over the kitchen island and placed them on it. Then he grabbed the wine from a nearby rack and the corkscrew from the island drawer. After popping the cork, Westram poured some of the liquid into both glasses.

Leaving the bottle on the island, Westram crossed to the table. He placed one before Arthur, who thanked him. The other he set in front of Noah. Unable to help himself, Westram took a second to press his lips to Noah's.

"I know you don't accept it quite yet," Westram murmured after lifting his head a few inches so he could peer into his mate's eyes. "But we'll get there." With an encouraging smile, Westram added, "I'm patient like that."

Westram heard Kaiser smother a snort, but he didn't comment on it. Instead, he returned to the kitchen. After handing off a beer to his alpha, he grabbed the pizza out of the refrigerator.

"Do you want to join us?" Westram asked his alpha. He also figured Noah would appreciate having his best friend at hand after all the fear, pain, and crazy that had taken over his life. "I have a pepperoni, too. I'll toss that in after the chicken is done."

"Sounds good," Kaiser replied before taking a swig of his

beer.

At the same time, Arthur nodded as he swallowed a sip of the wine.

Noah had done the same and hummed appreciatively. "Oh, this is one of my favorites," he stated, staring at Westram in surprise. Then his brows furrowed. "Have you been stocking your home with things for me?"

Unwilling to lie to his mate, Westram nodded while hitting buttons to pre-heat the oven. He crossed to the dining room table and settled in a chair beside Noah. Taking his free hand with his own, he squeezed lightly.

"Hope eternal," Westram whispered.

"That I'd come around," Noah finished.

Westram nodded again. "Yes, my mate."

Noah inhaled deeply, then let it out slowly between pursed lips. After eyeing Westram for a few more seconds, he turned his attention to Arthur. "You believe all this?"

Arthur nodded once. "Shall we prove shifting to you?" He peered at Kaiser. "Do you mind?"

Kaiser smiled indulgently at Arthur. "Of course, I don't mind, my love." Then he turned his intense, green-eyed gaze on Noah. "Did Westram and Anthony explain to you that you can never pass these secrets on to others? Friends or family?"

Even as Noah began to shake his head, he admitted, "I don't have any family, and you know my best friends." He waved his hand to indicate Arthur. Then he froze. "Wait." Noah's eyes narrowed. "Jacob doesn't know. Does he?"

"No, I never told Jacob," Arthur told him, his voice soothing. "If he comes here and finds his mate in one of Kaiser's shifters, we will then, but—" Arthur shrugged and shook his head. "Finding your paranormal mate is like finding the other half of your soul. It's not something I would want to tell him about, just to see him grow old and pass because he never found that. It would be . . . cruel."

Noah opened his mouth, then closed it again. Moving his focus to Westram, he stated, "That's what you meant by bonding. Isn't it?"

Westram massaged the hand he still held while choosing his words carefully. "A lot happens during bonding, so if you're talking about something specific, you'll need to say it." Seeing Noah struggling to put whatever he was thinking into words, Westram realized he and Anthony hadn't explained much about bonding, so he tried to help by saying, "When a human bonds with his shifter, his life is extended to match the shifters. Your aging will slow, Noah. Your bones will become stronger, so they're harder to break. Your healing will speed up. Your natural immunities to sickness will increase."

Pausing, Westram tried to figure out if he'd forgotten anything.

"Wow," Noah whispered.

"You forgot about a few things, huh?" Kaiser commented dryly.

Hearing the beep of the oven, signaling it had finished preheating, Westram sighed deeply as he rose. "There's so damn much," he grumbled as he stalked into the kitchen. After placing the pizza into the oven, Westram returned to the table.

Westram focused on Noah. "So, uh, did you have a particular thing you were actually asking about?" He'd just thrown a lot at his mate, and he looked a little shell-shocked.

Noah blinked a few times, then licked his lips. "Um, the age thing, I think." After taking a sip of his wine, he rubbed the back of his neck. "Okay, so, yeah. I get why no one can know." Grimacing, Noah stared at Arthur. "I guess it's easier to keep a secret from Jacob if you're rarely around, huh?"

Arthur's smile appeared sad. "Well, part of that is the fact that my mate is here." He indicated Kaiser.

Nodding, Noah sounded a little absent as he asked, "Do shifters always expect the human to move in with them?"

"Not always," Westram replied honestly. "But considering I'm a marine shifter, this is a safe place for me."

"Shifting," Noah whispered. Then he focused on Kaiser. "Okay. You said you could prove it. Will you?"

Kaiser nodded. "Of course." His smile appeared a bit tight around the edges of his lips. "Be aware, I turn into a colossal squid. I have the ability to partially shift my arms and legs into my animal's tentacles. *That* is what you will be seeing."

Noah nodded.

Sitting so close to Noah, Westram knew his mate still scented of disbelief.

That was made abundantly clear when, less than a minute later, Kaiser changed his left arm into a pair of tentacles, and Noah's eyes rolled to the back of his head. Westram barely caught him before he fell out of his chair.

Noah's mind replayed what he'd seen—Kaiser's arm turning into . . . things . . . even before he opened his eyes.

How is that possible?

Except, everyone had been telling him, over and over, *how* it was possible. The man wasn't human. He called himself a shifter—a paranormal being who could turn into an animal. According to Kaiser, that animal was a colossal squid.

Noah really didn't know what that type of squid looked like other than the basics—a body with big eyes, eight tentacles, and two longer feeding arms. The fact that the word *colossal* was in the name made him think the creature had to be pretty large. After all, Kaiser was a big, strong, buff guy.

So, what does that mean for Westram and the shark he claims to be?

"I know you're awake, my mate." Westram's soft voice whispered into his ear. "Remember, you're totally safe here. I'll never let anyone harm you again."

Needing explanations, Noah blinked open his eyes. "So,"

he whispered. "Everything you told me is true."

Westram threaded his fingers through Noah's hair, massaging his scalp lightly in the process. "Yes, Noah," he crooned. "I have never lied to you."

"Mates."

Cocking his head, Westram murmured, "That's not a question, but I'll respond with, yes. You're mine, and I'm yours." He leaned forward and pecked a kiss to his lips. "You're mine to please, to protect, to shower with every bit of love and respect I can think of."

"Damn," Noah muttered. When he saw Westram's brows furrow and a hint of hurt enter his expression, he grabbed the man's forearm. "I just . . . I've never had that before," he admitted. Grimacing, he told Westram, "I've always had shit luck with boyfriends. You—" Noah lifted his other hand, doing his best to ignore the way it trembled as he began to finger the other man's thick gray hair. "You're something I never expected, Westram." Snorting, he quickly added, "And I don't mean the turning into a shark part."

Westram sighed deeply as he nuzzled into Noah's petting. The look of bliss on his face caused just by Noah's touch to his hair, temple, and around his ear nearly took his breath away. His heartrate spiked for a new reason as realization filled him at how his touch affected the man.

Shifter.

Whatever.

To Noah's surprise, he suddenly found that he didn't care. He wanted to see more of the sweet looks of appreciation as well as experience the kindness and caring Westram bestowed upon him. Most of all, he wanted the kind of relationship the shifter seemed to be promising him.

Before Noah could figure out how to explain his desires, the beep of the oven filled the air.

Westram opened his eyes and smiled warmly at Noah. "That's the chicken pizza. Are you—"

Noah's stomach growled, and Westram chuckled.

"I'll take that as a yes," Westram murmured, leaning down and pecking Noah's lips in a too-short kiss. "Do you want to return to the table? I can cut the pizza and bring it out here. We can put on a movie." Westram indicated behind him to the dark TV screen.

Realizing he was lying on the sofa in the living room, Noah glanced around. "Um, what happened to Arthur and Kaiser?" he asked, a wash of embarrassment filling him.

Geez. I just fainted in front of all of them.

"We're here," Arthur said, his voice coming from somewhere beyond the backside of the sofa.

Right. The dining room.

"We just wanted to give you time to process when you woke." That was Kaiser. His deep voice held a wealth of understanding. "If you have questions, we'll answer them. If you need support from Arthur, we're still here. If you want privacy, we'll give you that, too."

"I want . . ." Noah began, then paused, uncertain what he wanted.

Then Noah's stomach growled again.

Westram chuckled, rising to his feet. "Pizza. You want pizza." Heading around the sofa, he disappeared from sight.

Noah listened, hearing a bit of rattling, scraping, and the soft squeak of the oven door opening and closing. Inhaling deeply, he reveled in the aroma of the pizza perfuming the air. His mouth watered, and he knew he really was hungry.

Easing to a sitting position, Noah scrubbed his hands over his face. He massaged his temples and rubbed under his glasses. Finally, he straightened.

It was time.

I need answers and dinner with my buddy and his husband and the hot guy who wants me will give them to me.

Easing to his feet, Noah made his way to the dining room. He spotted his forgotten wine glass, still half full, and picked it up. After gulping it down, he placed it back on the table.

Then Noah sat down, glancing between a concerned-looking Arthur and a stoic-faced Kaiser.

"Please stay," Noah urged. "I think I'd like you both here to help Westram answer questions." Then he scowled. "And I need to know if you've discovered anything more about Patrick."

The corners of Kaiser's lips turned up in a small smile. "Sounds good, Noah."

CHAPTER SIX

When Westram had been waiting for Noah to acknowledge their bond, he'd thought he'd been sexually frustrated. He'd been wrong. With Noah having been living in his apartment for the last three days, Westram thought he would go out of his mind with need.

Of course, never would he ever do anything that would pressure his mate.

Instead, Westram hopped into the shower each morning and took care of his morning wood—twice. Then he headed to the kitchen and started coffee and breakfast. He would load up a tray with plates of food, coffee for him, and orange juice for his mate.

Westram would then go to his bedroom with the tray. Every morning, Noah was awake and waiting for him. He would be sitting up in bed, having already cleaned up in the ensuite—Westram's sensitive hearing always allowed him to hear him.

The fourth morning started the same as the rest.

Taking the tray into the bedroom, Westram immediately noticed a change. His mate had the fingers of his good hand twisted in the comforter. Instead of watching the door, Noah was glaring at his bandaged right hand.

Placing the tray on the legs over Noah's lap, as usual, still didn't get his mate to look at him.

Unease slithered up Westram's spine. He eased onto the bed beside his mate, same as always. Then, after a second of hesitation, he changed his own pattern.

Instead of encouraging Noah to eat breakfast, Westram reached over and gently untwined his mate's fingers from the comforter. "Are you okay, my mate?" he asked softly, squeezing his human's slender fingers gently with his own much larger ones. "Did you receive bad news from a client or something?"

Westram had heard Noah typing away on his laptop while he'd been making breakfast. His mate had been so grateful to discover that Patrick hadn't screwed with his computer. The man obviously hadn't thought Noah would survive, so his equipment hadn't mattered.

"Um, or something," Noah murmured, finally turning to peer at him. Questions swam in his green eyes. "Did you know I've been lying in your bed for the last three nights, and you've refused to share it with me? Why?"

Shock infused Westram.

That had been the last thing he'd thought his mate would say.

"I-I—" Westram paused, stopping his stuttering. After clearing his throat, he whispered, "I thought I was giving you time to heal. Time to—"

"You held me when I was unconscious," Noah broke in, his brows furrowing as annoyance filled his tone and scent. "How is that any different than here?"

Westram realized suddenly that he hadn't asked Noah what he wanted. He'd just assumed. Blowing out a breath, he tightened his hold on Noah's hand when he tried to pull it free.

"I'm sorry for the misunderstanding," Westram began quickly. Reaching over with his free hand, he gripped his thigh. "I wanted to be here with you, but I made some bad assumptions." Bringing Noah's hand to his lips, Westram gently nibbled his knuckles. "Will you forgive me? Will you tell me what you want?"

Noah's nostrils flared, and his breathing sped up just a smidge.

Westram could smell his rising arousal. He could see it in the dilation of his mate's eyes. Even the way he blinked a couple of times betrayed his desires.

"I want to know why you thought holding me now, in your apartment, is any different than holding me while in my own bed."

Nodding slowly, Westram tried to figure out the right words. "Well, we sat at the table and explained shifters and our desires when it comes to mates and bonding," he began softly. He paused an instant, then continued, "You simply nodded . . . without saying anything, and I didn't know what that meant." Lifting his hand from Noah's thigh, Westram scratched the back of his neck. "I want to hold you and claim you with every fiber of my being." He pinned his mate with a heated gaze, letting him see the truth of his words. "If you had given me even one indication that you were interested in what we discussed at the table, that you were ready, I would have been all over you, Noah."

Noah opened his mouth, then closed it again. His brows furrowed as he shifted his gaze to where Westram held onto him. He swallowed so hard his Adam's apple bobbed.

Finally, Noah whispered, "I've never been the aggressor, Westram." He peered at him through his lashes. "I've always been the passive one. An attractive man would come onto me, and I'd go along with it. He just . . . assumed."

"And you assumed that's what would happen here," Westram murmured back, keeping his voice just as low, as intimate. Releasing Noah's hand, he eased closer to his mate so he could wrap that arm around him. Gently gripping his human's chin between his thumb and forefinger, Westram urged his head a bit higher so their gazes met fully. "I would never take something from you that was not freely given,

Noah. If you want me, tell me, and I will give you as much pleasure as you can possibly handle." Then Westram eased closer and pecked a kiss to Noah's lips. "From now until the end of our days."

Noah's lips parted, and he panted softly. He stared at Westram with a slightly vacant expression. Even a whimper erupted from Noah that caused a burn of desire to flare in Westram's gut.

I need this human so damn badly.

Then, the most wondrous thing happened.

"I want you, too," Noah whispered huskily. He tightened his hold on Westram's fingers while telling him, "I want what you're offering. So very badly. Will you show me?"

Noah waited with bated breath for Westram's response.

Over the last several days, he'd wondered when Westram would make his move. He'd figured he would give him a day, maybe two, to recover enough. Then he would pounce on him.

Instead, he'd done nothing.

Well, Westram *had* taken care of Noah, and while the touches were kind and gentle, he hadn't done anything beyond that. It had felt wonderful and excruciating all at the same time. Even though he'd experienced it so briefly, Noah had missed Westram's arms around him as he'd slept.

"Gods, yes, Noah," Westram murmured, his gray eyes turbulent as he peered down at him. "It would be the greatest honor of my life to have you beside me for the rest of our days."

Noah's heart thudded wildly in his chest as he stared back at Westram. He read the feral need that had been banked these last couple of days, and it caused his pulse to race. Lifting his good hand, he skimmed the pads of his fingertips up Westram's freshly shaven cheek, reveling in the way the man's lips parted slightly and his eyes slid to half-mast.

Never had a man looked at him as Westram was doing right then.

"So what are you waiting for?" Noah asked, feeling bold.

Westram turned his head and kissed Noah's palm. Returning his focus to his eyes, he leveled a hungry gaze upon him. "I take it you're not interested in breakfast?"

In truth, Noah had completely forgotten the tray of food and drink even though it lay across his lap.

Noah shook his head.

"Thank the gods," Westram growled, pulling away. "You smell so damn good all the time." While he grumbled the words, his pleasure in them could be heard loud and clear. Grabbing the tray, Westram moved it to the nightstand. "This can be reheated later."

Then Westram pulled open the nightstand's drawer and pulled something from it. When he tossed it onto the pillow beside him, Noah sucked in a gasp of anticipation. He yanked his focus away from the lube in time to see Westram whip his shirt over his head.

The hard lines and firm muscles revealed to Noah were a feast for the eyes. His soon-to-be lover was all smooth, bronzed flesh. The cut of his abdominals created a perfect vee that disappeared into his sweatpants enticingly.

Before Noah could get up the confidence to reach out and touch, Westram had shoved those down and off, too. When he straightened, he revealed his long, thick prick, standing tall and ready. The length jutting from his groin had to be at least eight inches and perfectly proportioned thickness.

Noah's chute clenched, but he knew it wasn't nerves. He anticipated what Westram could do with his endowment, and he could hardly wait. As Noah stared, a bead of pre-cum oozed from Westram's slit.

Westram groaned, drawing Noah's focus back to his face.

His handsome features were twisted in a mask of pleasure-pain. His cheeks were flushed, and his eyes were narrowed.

"The way you look at me, my mate," Westram whispered. "Gonna eat you up."

"Yes, please," Noah replied, a breathy quality to his voice that he'd never heard before.

"Mine," Westram growled, his voice deepening with that one word. At the same time, he grabbed the comforter and slowly drew it down. "Never gonna be alone again, my love."

Noah felt a shiver work up his spine at those words. "Yes, please," he repeated, because it was the only thing that he seemed to be able to think. Noah wanted every promise that appeared to glow in Westram's eyes.

"You're wearing way too many clothes, Noah," Westram purred, the bed dipping as he placed one knee on it beside Noah's hip. Reaching for the hem of Noah's shirt, Westram asked, "May I remove this?"

Immediately, Noah lifted his arms.

Westram lifted it, tugging it over his head. With a gentle touch, he maneuvered the fabric off his injured hand last. Then he dropped the shirt off the side of the bed.

Sliding his gaze over Noah's revealed torso, Westram hummed appreciatively. "You're stunning." At the same time, he skimmed over the still-healing cuts that Patrick had inflicted. "I'm going to trace my tongue over every one of these marks," Westram told him. Before Noah could ask why, he met his gaze and explained, "That will speed up the healing."

"Why didn't you do that before?" Noah asked, unable to contain his curiosity.

A pinched smile tightened the corners of Westram's lips. "It would have started the bonding process, and I would never do that without your permission."

Noah understood. "You're an honorable man, Westram."

Westram's features loosened, the lust returning. "Thank you, my mate." Turning his attention to Noah's sleep shorts, he stated, "Time to take these off." Westram rested his hand above his braced knee. "It might hurt a little, but I'll do my best to keep the pain to a minimum."

"I know you will," Noah replied, having complete faith in Westram. He'd already proven how caring he was with Noah's healing body.

With a pleased smile, Westram climbed onto the bed. He helped Noah slide down until he was sprawled in the middle, his shifter strength making the maneuver easy. After that, he pulled the shorts from him, easing them off his damaged leg. Then Westram bent and pressed a kiss to the skin above the brace.

"I'm so sorry you were hurt," Westram murmured with a sigh. Lifting his gaze to Noah, he grumbled, "We'll find that fucker. He'll never get near you again."

Noah didn't want to think about Patrick right then. He knew the man had fled. Dare and Pisces had only found Patrick's empty home and the *Prius* left in the garage.

Cupping Westram's jaw, Noah smiled at him. "I know you will." Then he pointed at his naked groin, since Westram had removed his underwear along with the shorts. "But I think something else is more important right now. Don't you?"

Westram's grin appeared a little feral. "Oh, yeah."

Except, instead of focusing on Noah's prick, Westram levered over him. He threaded his fingers into his hair and took his mouth in a plundering kiss. Westram didn't ask permission. He demanded, thrusting his tongue into his mouth, lapping and teasing their appendages together.

By the time Westram ended the onslaught, Noah's lungs were screaming for air even as his head swam in heady bliss. His body felt heated from the inside out. He arched beneath Westram's caressing touches as the man skimmed his other hand all over him.

Westram's mouth followed his hand, mapping him with his lips and tongue. Doing exactly as he'd said he would, he licked and kissed over every mark Noah's sadistic attacker had left behind. Following Westram's tongue, prickles of pleasure were left in their wake.

"Oh, Wes," Noah whined, trembles working through him as Westram began easing down his torso. The hairs on his arms stood on end from the pleasure of his lover's touches and kisses. He couldn't control the way his stomach trembled as Westram traced his fingertips over his flesh. Even his legs twitched and jerked spastically, and despite the pain it caused, his throbbing erection didn't soften one iota.

Westram hummed before suckling gently at one nipple.

Arching into the sweet ministrations, Noah called Westram's name. The light pulls shot straight to his groin, and his cock throbbed. When Westram moved to the other bud and gave it the same treatment, he felt his balls tighten, and he feared he would come untouched.

Somehow, Westram knew. He moved off his nipple and began working over Noah's torso. At the same time, he grabbed the lube and poured some onto his fingers.

Noah watched the move with anticipation, knowing what was to come and wanting it so badly.

"You're mine, Noah," Westram murmured against the flesh covering his ribcage. Holding his gaze, he licked over a mark before demanding, "Say it."

Feeling the tell-tale tingle from Westram's saliva healing him, Noah barely managed to formulate words. "I-I—" He paused, swallowed hard, then tried again. "I'm yours, Westram. All yours."

"Damn straight," Westram claimed on a growl.

Then Westram slid one finger deep into Noah's channel.

Groaning at the exquisite stretch, Noah let the tremble take him. His entire body felt as if he'd stuck his finger in a light socket, except in a good way. Prickles danced across his skin, caused by Westram's fingers and mouth. The hairs on his limbs stood on end, and shivers of delight racked his senses. With the way Westram massaged his inner walls, teasing and grazing his prostate with every few thrusts, Noah felt his dick throb and pulse, the tickle of pre-cum sliding over his crown causing his balls to draw up.

When Westram reached Noah's groin and swallowed his shaft to the root, it was game over.

Losing control of his body completely, Noah arched and screamed. His orgasm crashed over his system like a tsunami wave. He felt the sucking pulls on his dick and the pressure in his ass, and called out Westram's name over and over.

Finally, Westram released his shaft with a wet slurp, and Noah managed to peel open eyelids he couldn't recall closing.

Noah panted harshly, his senses still floating from the best damn orgasm he'd ever experienced. As he watched Westram wipe his mouth with the back of his hand, it didn't hide the smug grin on his lips. His eyes gleamed with satisfaction.

Then Westram eased his fingers from Noah's channel and levered over him, gripping himself and stroking his meat in the process, greasing himself up.

"That was just the beginning, my mate," Westram claimed.

"I-I don't th-think you can top that," Noah managed to get out.

Westram rested his weight on his slick fingers, obviously not caring about the sheets. Holding Noah's gaze, he touched his cock head to Noah's prepared hole.

"I'll take that challenge, my mate."

Then Westram surged into Noah's chute and made good on his promise, ringing two more orgasms, each better than the last, from Noah's body — one from pegging his prostate and another from his claiming bite.

CHAPTER SEVEN

Nothing could start Westram's day off better than waking with Noah cuddled in his arms. Although, the way his mate was subtly rocking his ass against his groin was a damn close second. Sliding his palm down from Noah's stomach to his groin, Westram fisted his mate's morning erection.

Rutting against Noah's plush cheeks, Westram pressed his prick into his crack. "Good morning, my mate," he purred into his lover's ear before nipping the lobe.

Noah hummed and turned his head a little, peering at him out of the corner of his eye.

Westram could just see that his sweet mate's lips were curved into a mischievous smile.

"It would be a much better morning if you slid your thick piece of meat into me."

Growling softly, Westram felt his excitement spike. He reached behind him and grabbed the ever-present lube from off the nightstand. They rarely bothered to put it away.

As Westram drew away from Noah just enough to squirt some onto his hand so he could grease himself up, he reveled in how Noah's naturally playful character was beginning to appear. His mate could be sassy and sweet as well as demanding and fiery. Westram loved every aspect of him . . . especially how his lover was starting to ask for what he needed.

And I will always give it to him.

Westram dropped the lube on the comforter as he eased his finger into Noah's hole. Listening to Noah murmur, "More," and finding him still a bit stretched from their love-play the night before, Westram obeyed, sinking in a second finger. That was quickly followed by a third.

"Yessss," Noah hissed, rocking his hips, welcoming his touch. "Now, Wes. I'm ready."

Fully on board with that, Westram eased his fingers out of Noah's body. He quickly greased up his dick and lined himself up. Then, in one long, smooth glide, Westram sank balls deep into his mate.

Sighing deeply, Westram stilled with his erection buried inside Noah. He gripped his mate's hip, holding him still. With the front of his body flush to Noah's back from chest to calves, Westram took a few heartbeats to just revel in the feel of joining with his mate.

"I love you so damn much, Noah," Westram whispered, unable to hold in the declaration. "Thank you so much for accepting me."

When Noah peered over his shoulder at him, a soft smile curved his lips. "And I'm so damn lucky to have you, too."

A mischievous glint entered Noah's green eyes, and Westram felt his lover's chute muscles clamp onto his cock once, twice, giving him a sensual massage.

"Time to move, my shifter," Noah ordered.

Westram groaned as he buried his face in the crook of Noah's neck. "You feel so perfect," he mumbled, but he did as his mate asked. "So amazing."

With his left hand under Noah's body and curved up to hold his torso, Westram moved the other to his hip. He held him steady as he eased his cock from the cocoon of Noah's warm body. As his crown teased against his mate's guardian muscle, he reversed directions, driving back into him.

Feeling the heat of Noah's body encasing him again, Westram groaned his pleasure. He'd never felt anything as exquisite as this human, and he knew he never would. He never wanted to, either.

As Westram picked up his pace, driving into Noah over and over, he adjusted the angle of his ruts each time. When his mate cried out and a shudder went through his body, he knew he'd found it. Westram sought out that same spot each time he stabbed into his man, driving his lover's pleasure higher.

When Noah's cries turned to whimpers, Westram knew he was close. He loved how vocal his mate was and wanted to hear more. Westram wanted everything.

Moving his hand to Noah's cock, Westram began jacking him in time with his thrusts. In less than a minute, the walls encasing his length tightened, and his mate's scream of ecstasy filled the room. He continued to milk his lover while half-rutting, rubbing his cock head against that stimulating gland within him.

Westram felt Noah's shudders begin to taper off and heard his moans switch to whines, telling him of the sensitivity of the cock in his hand.

Unable to stave off his own release any longer, Westram growled as his balls pulled tight. His senses sang as his bliss crested. In ecstasy-inducing spurts, he poured his seed into his lover.

Seeing the way Noah bowed his head just a little, Westram took the invitation. He sank his canines into his claiming mark, reopening the wound. His mate's delicious life-giving fluid filled his mouth. His own moans of delight mixed with Noah's, and he felt his mate's channel squeeze him once more, telling him he'd come again. The sweet pressure drew several more bursts of seed from Westram's balls, and his mind reeled with his pleasure.

Westram eased his teeth from Noah's neck. He licked over the mark, sealing it once more. Sighing, he nuzzled his nose along his nape, floating on the afterglow.

For several long minutes, they lay together, not talking, just enjoying the intimacy and post-coital cuddling.

Okay. This is the best way to start the day.

"Are you feeling up to a tour of the marine park?" Westram asked. He sat next to his mate at the dining room table, drinking a morning cup of coffee. Noah had just finished his juice and blueberry bagel with cream cheese.

Noah relaxed in his chair, his left leg propped on a pillow on a chair kitty-corner to him. "Yeah. I'd like to get out of the house." His face flushed a little as he hurriedly added, "Not that I haven't loved nesting in here with you."

Westram grinned, not at all offended. "I've loved it, too." Winking, he threaded his fingers with Noah's. "But I'm normally a pretty active guy, so I'm getting a little stir-crazy, too."

Relief filling his features, Noah smiled. "Okay."

They were still working on their communication.

"Do you need to catch up on any work first?" Westram asked as he rose to his feet and grabbed their plates. He knew Noah had spent hours on his laptop, responding to clients and playing catch-up after missing a weeks' worth of messages. "I can check in with Eban if you do."

Westram and Kaiser had explained their pod's hierarchy to Noah, so he hoped he remembered who that was. Eban was their shifter group's head enforcer. The alpha had given Westram the week off, but if Noah was going to go back to a regular work schedule, he planned to as well.

No point sitting at home twiddling my thumbs while Noah is working, even if I do love being so near to him.

Noah shook his head. "While I should really spend a few hours on expense reports this afternoon, I'd like to get some fresh air this morning." Pointing outside, he commented, "The day looks gorgeous out there."

Westram silently agreed. The sky was blue with only a few puffy white clouds marring the view. His sensitive hearing could make out the crash of the surf through the open kitchen window. The scent of the ocean filled his nostrils.

A perfect day.

"Then let's get dressed, and we'll head out."

Westram handed Noah his cane, then helped him to his feet. While their bonding had helped speed up his mate's healing, it didn't fix strained ligaments overnight. Noah would need to use a cane and brace for at least another week.

"Didn't the doc say swimming was good therapy for your knee?" Westram asked curiously.

Noah nodded. "Yeah. You wanna go swimming?"

"There's a private beach a little ways north of here," Westram told him. "There's some great snorkeling there, plus I could show you my shark."

Westram hadn't pushed the subject, but his shark was eager to meet their mate.

Noah paused in the doorway to their bedroom. The scent of his unease filled the air. "Um, is it safe?"

Wrapping his arms around Noah's waist, Westram smiled down at him. "Totally safe, my love," he assured. "My shark is still me, just in a different form."

Nodding once, although he still scented of uncertainty, Noah agreed. "Okay."

Westram knew his mate would believe him once he had a chance to swim with him.

Noah figured Westram could scent his nerves. He'd explained how shifters could determine certain emotions through scent. They could even detect lies and arousal, too.

That could get embarrassing.

Still, Westram took him at his word and they dressed for a day of swimming, snorkeling, and picnicking. Carrying the picnic basket in one hand with a blanket draped over that shoulder, he rested his other hand on the small of Noah's back. He guided him out of their complex to the parking lot and to a large pick-up truck.

Smirking, Noah waved at it in amusement. "Why am I not surprised?"

Westram cocked his head. "What do you mean?"

Noah realized his lover wasn't following. Smiling indulgently, he handed over the bag of supplies he'd had to talk Westram into letting him carry. Otherwise, his shifter would have insisted on carrying everything.

"I mean, you're this huge, brawny, six-foot-four guy, so of course you're gonna have a big truck."

Chuckling, Westram shrugged as he placed everything into the backseat of the quad cab machine. "What can I say?" He turned and winked, shutting the door behind him. "I need the legroom."

As Noah chuckled, Westram opened the passenger side door for him.

"You know I'm not a girl. Right?"

Westram's gaze turned lascivious as he gave Noah a heated once-over. "Oh, my mate." His voice was husky as he gripped Noah's upper arm with one hand and his nape with the other. "I know exactly what you have between your legs." Moving the hand from his arm to blatantly cup Noah's crotch, Westram fondled his prick through his board shorts, drawing a harsh gasp from him. "Do I need to explore again to remind you how much I love what you're packin'?"

Noah couldn't help but buck into Westram's ministrations. The delicious tingles he created with his expert hand were just too spine-tingling to resist. His breathing sped up, and a whine escaped him as he felt his cock lengthen.

Just as Noah was going to say, "Yes, please," he heard the distinctive sound of a child laughing.

"Shit," Noah hissed, jerking away from Westram. "We're in public!"

Westram nodded. "That we are." He grinned, completely unabashed. "Let's go somewhere more private."

Noah allowed Westram to help him into the cab, but he drew the line at the man buckling his seatbelt. He wasn't helpless, after all. Of course, seeing Westram's pout almost had him changing his mind, but he stood firm.

After closing Noah's door, Westram jogged around the front of the vehicle. As his lover drove the truck out of the lot, Noah spotted the child he'd heard. A girl of about six swung between the hands of a man and a woman — probably her parents — giggling and grinning.

Damn. I've never forgotten myself like that. Shifter mating sure can make you forget yourself.

Instead of turning in the direction of the marine park, Westram headed north.

"Is it far?" Noah asked curiously.

Westram shook his head. "Naw. Just up the road."

Noah felt a fissure of unease as they left the safety of the shifter run facilities. "Is it safe?"

Dare, Pisces, and Ovram still hadn't tracked down Patrick, yet.

Resting his hand on Noah's thigh, Westram stated, "I would never let anything happen to you, my mate." Before Noah could tell Westram that he didn't want anything to happen to him, either, Westram added, "But this is still our property. It's gated and monitored with security cameras." Then he chuckled. "Well, the approach and some of the area is." Westram winked, and his smile turned roguish. "The beach is *not* monitored for obvious reasons."

"Is this a nude beach?" Noah asked on a gasp.

Westram lifted his hand and made a so-so gesture. "It's a private beach owned by shifters, so . . . yeah." He shrugged as he added, "There's definitely a possibility of running into naked people down here."

Noah felt his cheeks heat just at the idea. He'd never considered himself a prude, but he'd never been tempted to go to a nude beach either. There were some parts of other people he just didn't need to see.

Then Westram growled softly as he paused at a gate. "However." He reached over and threaded their fingers together. "If there are others there, do not undress in front of them. Shifters are only naked for a short time before and after a shift."

Understanding dawned, and Noah nodded. "So, clothes are always on hand."

Westram nodded. "For the most part, or if not, and the shifter realizes one is a human mate, they'll head into the water for decencies' sake."

Noah nodded. "Okay."

Then Westram released him so he could turn and enter a code into the box out the window. The gate opened, and Westram started the truck forward again.

"How many people have the gate code?" Noah asked curiously. He rubbed at his arms. Maybe he was being paranoid, but he had the same feeling as the last time he'd felt as if he were being watched.

"Each person has an individual code," Westram told him. "That way Ovram can monitor who's at the beach, although some swim to it in animal form. This way, no one from the outside can get in." With his brows furrowing, Westram glanced Noah's way. "Why?"

Rubbing the back of his neck, Noah mumbled, "I'm probably just being paranoid. Sorry."

"Always trust your instincts, Noah," Westram told him. "What are you thinking?"

"Just that I felt like I was being watched."

Westram hummed as he pushed a button on the steering wheel. The unmistakable sound of a phone ringing sounded through the cab. A second later, someone answered.

"Hey, Wes," a deep voice greeted. "What's up?"

"Hey, Ov," Westram responded, letting Noah know who he'd called. "Any word on Patrick?"

"Only that he's no longer in San Diego," Ovram told him. "The guy's gone underground." With a sigh, he added, "It would help if Noah knew how they were connected."

"I wish I knew that, too," Noah admitted, announcing his presence.

"Hey, Noah," Ovram greeted. "Don't worry, man. We'll find him." Scoffing, he added, "And if Patrick finds you, just jump in the ocean. Everyone here knows who you are to Westram and will keep you safe." With a cold chuckle, Ovram claimed, "We'll make your attacker go swimmin' with the fishes."

As Noah let out a relieved chuckle, Westram wrapped up the call.

CHAPTER EIGHT

Westram noticed Noah appeared a little green from the steep drive down the side of the cliff to the lower parking area. He'd heard it was tough the first few times for mates, but there was no way he was going to make Noah walk down all the stairs.

"We're safe, my mate," Westram crooned as he exited the vehicle. "I've driven down this before. It's a bright, beautiful day. Plus, I would never put you in danger."

Noah took a deep breath, let it out through pursed lips, then followed that up by doing it again. He nodded even as he continued his deep breathing. By the time Westram rounded the vehicle and opened Noah's door, he looked and scented a little calmer.

Westram helped him from the truck, waiting until he got his balance on his cane. Then he guided him across the sand. After pecking a kiss to his lips, Westram ordered, "Wait here. I'll grab everything."

After Noah nodded, Westram returned to the truck. He placed the strap of the duffel bag over his shoulder. Picking up the blanket in one hand and the picnic basket in the other, he used his hip to bump the door closed.

Returning to where Noah waited—his focus on the sea's rolling waves—Westram placed the basket and bag on the sand. He spread out the blanket before moving the heavier items on top of it. That way, if a breeze kicked up, it wouldn't get blown away.

Stepping up behind Noah, Westram wrapped his arms

around him. He nuzzled his temple against his mate's. When Noah rested his hands over Westram's, he sighed deeply, happier than he'd ever been in his life.

"It's a little hypnotic, isn't it?" Westram whispered.

Noah nodded. "Yeah. Gorgeous, though."

"Definitely."

"Do you know what would really be gorgeous?"

Upon hearing the slightly familiar voice over the sound of the waves, Westram turned his head. He didn't miss the way Noah stiffened in his arms. When he spotted the blond striding across the sand toward him, he understood why.

"Hello, Patrick," Westram greeted. He'd wondered at his mate's sudden show of nerves, but it made sense now. Into Noah's ear, Westram murmured, "I wonder if you're a smidge clairvoyant, my mate."

"Just lived alone for so long in the city," Noah whispered back. "That my senses are honed for danger."

"Hmmm," Westram mused. "Do you remember what Ovram told you?" As he spoke, he urged Noah to take a step forward . . . toward the waves.

Noah resisted at first. "He was serious?"

"Oh, yeah."

"You may as well stop," Patrick yelled. "You have nowhere to go." He pulled a gun from his belt and began to cackle like a bad *Bond* villain. "Come now, and I'll make it quick. If not, I'll put a few holes in you and leave you to be carried out by the tide. I'm sure there are any number of fish that would be attracted by your bloody body."

"Neither of those options work for me," Westram hollered back, urging Noah to continue moving. Wondering if he could get the man talking to buy time, he commented, "Although, I am wondering how you got through the gate. Or did you leave your car on the street?"

Either way, Westram knew Ovram would notice damn

fast.

Patrick stopped twenty-five feet away, just outside lunging range, even for a shifter. "I've been watching your compound, and when I saw it was you in the truck, I followed you." Grinning maniacally, he commented, "Imagine my surprise when you come to such a lovely remote location. Getting the gate code while watching through binoculars was easy."

"Ahhhh . . ." Westram murmured. He felt the splash of the chilly water through his shoes. That meant an alarm would sound on Ovram's system, telling him that Westram's code had been entered twice. Dipping his head, Westram whispered for Noah's ears alone, "Cavalry will be here momentarily."

"How do we keep from getting shot until then?" Noah asked.

Good question.

"Shut up and get over here, Noah," Patrick screamed.

Noah took another step into the water while claiming, "I really have no idea who you are." Shaking his head, he continued, "In fact, I didn't even know your name was Patrick until Westram told me." Then he took another step deeper.

Patrick glared, his lips curling, and began to follow them. "You lying sack of shit," he screamed. "I know Benny told you about me."

"Benny?" Westram and Noah repeated the name at the same time.

Evidently, Noah recognized it, though, for he continued, "Do you mean Benson Suelman?"

"Of course, I mean that Benson," Patrick stated sarcastically. "How many Bennys have you dated?" Sneering, he added, "And don't lie that he didn't tell you about me. He was mine before he was yours. He came back to me, but you still managed to ruin everything."

Westram tried to keep Noah moving, but his mate's confusion seemed to have him frozen in place.

"What do you mean?" Noah seemed genuinely concerned. "He left me to return to his ex. I guess that was you." He waved toward Patrick. "I never talked to him again. I didn't ruin anything."

"He couldn't get over you!" Patrick screamed, lifting his gun. "So he killed himself."

Heaving Noah toward the deeper waves, Westram followed him into the water, doing his best to cover him. He heard the blast of the weapon being discharged and felt the pain of a slug hitting his upper back. A second later, more pain blossomed in his lower left side.

Then the water covered them. Ignoring the pain, Westram urged Noah to stay underwater and swim. Seeing that Noah was obeying, Westram gritted his teeth and shifted, all the while praying that if the bullets were still in his body, they wouldn't end up in some odd place in shark form.

Noah finally had his answers. He just wished he wasn't being shot at to get them. Never in a million years would he have connected the Patrick his ex-boyfriend had mentioned in passing, once, with the Patrick who'd attacked him.

After Benson had left him, Noah had immediately gone on a cruise with Arthur and Jacob. Seeing as they hadn't been together all that long, it hadn't taken much to get over him. Just another ex in the long line of exes who hadn't been worth his time.

Staying underwater, Noah swam as swiftly as he could toward the deep water. He had to trust that his lover would keep him safe way out there. Noah had heard plenty of tales of people going too deep, getting caught in rip tides, and being dragged out to sea.

The churning and bubbling of the water behind Noah caught his attention. He paused and curled in the water.

Turning, he tried to see what was happening.

When a grayish-brown shark with a long, serrated-looking nose appeared from the depths, Noah reeled back in shock. He almost screamed. Spotting the red drifting from the long, slender creature's sides, he froze.

Is this Westram? Has he been shot?

The animal swam by Noah, then circled back to him. The large gray eye stared at him as he passed before it changed direction and passed him again. As the beast circled him, Noah recognized the unmistakable sight of bullet wounds.

By then, Noah needed air. He tried kicking to the surface, but his wet, heavy clothes weighed him down. His brace made proper swimming difficult, and he flailed, struggling.

Noah felt the shark slide under him, slotting between his legs. To his shock, the creature began to head to the surface. Grabbing the dorsal fin, Noah rode the saw-shark up and up — *when did I go so deep* — until his head broke the surface of the waves.

Sucking in a much-needed lungful of air, Noah released the shark. The creature didn't go far. In fact, any time Noah began to struggle, the beast bumped him, offering support for a few seconds as it passed him.

Cackling from not far away drew Noah's attention. He peered toward the shore, seeing that he had to be at least seventy feet away. Still, he managed to hear Patrick's shouts over the roar of the ocean.

"I shot your boyfriend," Patrick yelled. "Did that shark eat him?" He laughed manically. "You're gonna be next."

Then Patrick aimed his gun at him in the water.

Noah felt a fissure of fear surge through him. He didn't know if he should dodge left or right. If he ducked underwater, he wasn't certain if he would be able to surface again.

Can the bullets travel through water?

He didn't know anything about guns.

The sound of the gun's report echoed through the air followed by a splash five feet to Noah's left.

Damn. That was close.

As Noah watched, Patrick took aim again.

Except, he didn't get another shot off. Like something out of a horror movie, a massive tentacle slithered from the depths and wrapped around him. It lifted Patrick into the air and shook him like a rag doll, making him drop the gun even as the man's horrified screams rent the air.

Then the tentacle swung in a broad arc. It released its hold on Patrick, sending him sailing through the air. Patrick landed with a splash about fifty feet away.

Unable to help himself, Noah ducked under the water and peered around. He spotted the fully clothed man doing his best to rise to the surface. Blooms of red swirled around him, telling Noah that there must have been barbs in the tentacle.

A squid.

Then the massive creature itself drifted into view.

Once again, Noah's natural reaction was to scream and swim away. Then he remembered.

Kaiser and William are squid shifters.

As Noah watched, the beast wrapped a tentacle around one of Patrick's legs. Another squid, nearly as large but shaped a bit differently, appeared on Patrick's other side. It wrapped a tentacle around Patrick's opposite arm.

The pair pulled in opposite directions, spreading the man. Just when Noah wondered if they intended to tear Patrick limb from limb, he spotted the saw-shark.

The shark surged through the water, moving shockingly fast. As the shark swam past Patrick's head, it flicked his own to the side. A bloom of red erupted from Patrick's neck . . . then the head floated away from the body.

Bile burned the back of Noah's throat, and he once again tried to break the surface. Except, his clothes were too heavy. He flailed.

Noah couldn't stop the scream when a tentacle wrapped around his waist. The hold was loose, and he suddenly found himself only waist-deep in the water. A soft lowing sound carried through the air to Noah, and he managed to shut his mouth upon hearing the soothing crooning noise.

Gaping, Noah stared at the huge animal holding him steady in the water. The beast's massive gray eye watched him unblinkingly. That was when Noah saw the intelligence within its depths.

"Holy shit," Noah whispered. Unable to help himself, he repeated, "Holy shit!"

The squid lowed again.

Noah didn't know if it was his imagination, but he thought there was a note of amusement in the sound.

To his left, the other squid surfaced.

He glanced between them, marveling at the craziness of the situation.

Before Noah could wrap his mind around that, he spotted a dorsal fin. To his surprise, the tentacle moved him toward it. Recognizing it as Westram's saw-shark, when it came close enough, Noah wrapped his arms around it.

The shark swam slowly toward shore, the squid keeping pace.

When his feet touched the sand, Noah let go. The shark turned, returning to deeper water. As he watched, the same odd bubbling appeared several yards away.

Then Westram rose from the water. He swiftly closed the distance between them and pulled Noah into his arms. "Are you okay?" Westram demanded, but before Noah could answer, he took his mouth in a deep, plundering, searching kiss.

Noah wrapped his arms around Westram and clung. He slid his arms up, intending to dig his hands into his lover's shoulder blades. Except, then Westram yanked his mouth away and groaned.

"What is it?" Noah cried.

"Sorry," Westram mumbled, panting. With a wry smile, he admitted, "Hit my wound."

"Wound?" Noah frowned. "What wound?"

"The idiot allowed himself to get shot," William commented with a snort. "Come to shore. Doc's on his way."

Then William gripped Westram's upper arm and placed a hand on Noah's back. He urged them both toward shore.

Kaiser hurried past them. When his naked ass appeared above the waves, Noah did his best to avert his gaze. Still, how could he not notice that it was a fine ass . . . although he thought Westram had a much nicer one.

Grabbing their discarded bag, Kaiser began rifling through it. He pulled out towels and spare shorts.

Noah took the shorts and began to help Westram into them. Unfortunately, the second he tried to bend, agony spiked through his body, reminding him of his own injuries. Losing his balance, he began to topple.

"Hey. Easy," Kaiser rumbled, catching him. "Have a seat. I'll help him."

Letting Kaiser place him on the blanket, Noah discovered with some relief that the alpha now had one of the towels they'd packed wrapped around his waist. William did, too.

After Westram donned the shorts, he settled on the blanket beside Noah. He took his good hand, threading their fingers together. Then he smiled wanly at him.

"That wasn't how I wanted to introduce you to my shark."

Noah heard the hesitation and worry in Westram's voice. Understanding from where it stemmed, he thought about the best way to reassure him. After all, Noah knew shifter justice was a little different than human justice.

Patrick had gone after Noah, Westram's mate, twice. His life was forfeit.

Deciding to go with something simple, Noah squeezed his

lover's hand and shrugged. "You have a nice shark."

Both the brothers laughed, and William patted Noah on the shoulder. "You'll fit in nicely, Noah. Welcome to the family."

Lifting his gaze to the brothers, Noah grinned. "Thanks. It's nice to have family."

Then Noah curled into Westram's side and waited for the doc to arrive so he could look them over . . . again.

"Let's not make a habit of this," Noah stated, leveling a serious gaze at Westram.

Westram nodded. "Let's not."

Then Westram kissed him, and that was good enough for Noah.

Excerpt

"Hey, Drew," Jillian called. "Got a sec?"

Fighting back a cringe, Drew turned and pasted a smile on his lips. "Sure. What can I help you with?" he asked, keeping his voice level and professional as he watched Jillian hurry to his side.

"It looks like there was a mix-up in scheduling," Jillian stated, nibbling her bottom lip. "There's a young man here that was supposed to see Mister Mindrid today, but he's not in." Her brows were furrowed, yet still she lifted her hand to her chest, teasing her fingertips along the neckline of her shirt.

Drew figured she meant to be provocative, but it was completely lost on him.

"Mister Litman is already with a client," Jillian continued, her lips curving into a fake-concerned moue. "I know you're supposed to be off after Mister Lucre leaves, but do you have time for a consultation?"

Even if Drew had had plans, he would never leave a client

hanging because someone — probably Jillian — had messed up scheduling.

"Certainly," Drew replied. "I'll need to finish with Mister Lucre first. Can they wait?" Another thought struck him. "Are they okay with seeing a different physical therapist?"

Jillian glanced back toward the lobby, hesitating.

Drew clenched his jaw for a second before taking a calming breath. Except, his lungs were filled with a cloying floral scent.

Ugh. Too much perfume again.

"I'll be back out shortly, Jillian," Drew told her, taking a step away. "If they're okay with a different therapist and are willing to wait, I'll pick them up then."

Then Drew pivoted and headed into the break room. He grabbed a bottle of water and swigged several gulps. After a glance at his watch, he saw he had a couple more minutes before returning to Ned.

Drew settled on a chair and stretched his legs out in front of him. Tipping his head, he rested it on the cushion. He focused on his breathing and relaxing the muscles of his neck and shoulders.

After a few minutes, Drew felt better. "Good thing tomorrow is Saturday," he muttered as he rose back to his feet. "Barbeque tonight at Jake's, and I know he'll let me crash there. Then a run with him in the morning."

Smiling, Drew headed back to Ned. "Feeling better?" he asked with a grin as he grabbed a towel.

"Getting better all the time," Ned replied, taking the towel.

To Drew's relief, his client sounded it, too.

After helping Ned from the hot tub and into the wheelchair, Drew took him to the changing room. "Don't forget to set up an appointment with Jillian for Monday," he reminded. After receiving confirmation from Ned, he left the man to it.

Drew returned to the front. Pausing at the opening, he swept his gaze around the area. His focus landed on the two waiting in the chairs there.

From the fact that the young man—a teenager around the age of fifteen—sported a large walking cast, Drew figured he was the client. He guessed the black-haired man with him would be his father. Then the adult turned his attention from the teenager and met his gaze.

Sucking in a shocked gasp, Drew peered into vibrant green eyes that had haunted his dreams for over six years.

"Will."

Will Hanson had given Drew his first kiss from a guy. While he indulged in one-night stands, he didn't kiss them—not anymore. Every time he'd kissed a trick, he'd been turned off. The memory of Will's soft lips pressed against his own slammed into Drew, causing his gut to clench and his mouth to tingle with sensory recall.

Rising to his feet, Will narrowed his eyes and swept his gaze over Drew. His expression said it all. He was trying to place him.

Damn. He doesn't remember me.

Drew sure as hell remembered Will. His thick black hair was longer than it had been in college, but he'd retained his lean runner's build. Back then, Will had worn black-rimmed glasses, but he wasn't wearing them now, making his green eyes seem even more vibrant.

Then Will's eyes widened a little, and his lips parted. "Drew?" he questioned softly. "Drew Menard?"

Unable to help himself, Drew grinned broadly. "Hey." He closed the distance between them, needing to get closer. "It's been years." Wanting to touch, Drew held out his hand. "How are you?"

Will hesitated an instant, then took Drew's hand. "Um, good. I'm good."

Drew felt Will's warm palm slide against his own, and he tightened his grip just a little. He wanted to hold onto the man. The urge to cradle Will's hand with his second one filled him, so he did it.

"Glad to hear it, Will. Really glad." Unable to help himself,

Drew added, "We need to meet for coffee. Catch up."

Drew knew he needed to rein in his excitement at seeing his college crush again—and so out of the blue. His cock was already thickening in his slacks, and his pants weren't going to hide his excitement for long.

"Mister Hanson," a young masculine voice murmured.

Will pulled his hand from Drew's as he half-turned in the teenager's direction. "Pete, this is Mister Menard." With a glance Drew's way, he offered with a half-smile, "Sorry I didn't make the connection when the receptionist said you were available to talk to us." Before Drew could reassure the man, Will continued, "This is Pete Skarner."

Using his big head, Drew turned his attention to Pete. "Hey, buddy." He gave the young man an encouraging smile. "Looks like you got yourself into a little trouble, huh?"

Pete scowled at Drew as he rolled his eyes. "Wasn't my fault."

"It never is," Drew countered, shoving his hands into his pockets. If his hands were out of the way, maybe he could control his urge to touch Will again. "So, let's head back to my office to talk." Realizing he needed a bit more information, he turned and peered at Jillian. "Do you have Pete's file?"

Jillian nodded as she held up a file. "Right here." As she spoke, she rested one arm on her desk and leaned forward, using the move to push her boobs forward.

Drew kept his focus squarely on Jillian's face as he plucked the file from her fingers. "Thank you." Then he turned his attention back to Will and Pete. Drew saw Will helping Pete to his feet and offered, "I can get you a wheelchair if you need a break from those crutches."

Pete scowled at him. "I got it."

Great. Due to some error, I get to handle a belligerent teenager. Swell.

At least Pete's attitude caused Drew's arousal to ease.

Forcing himself to keep a professional smile on his face, Drew nodded. "Of course. Standard procedure to offer." He started walking. "If you'll both join me."

Drew led the way deeper into the clinic. When he passed Ned crutching his way to the front, he clapped him lightly on the upper arm. "See you Monday, Ned."

"Yep. Thanks, Drew."

Pointing his finger at Ned, Drew reminded him, "And don't forget what we discussed." That was all he could say in front of other clients.

Ned fixed him with a wry grin. "Yeah. Yeah."

Laughing lightly, Drew opened the door a few feet away. He led the way inside and indicated the chairs opposite his desk. Once they'd entered and headed that way, Drew closed the door and rounded his desk.

As Drew placed the file before him, he settled in his own chair. Glancing between Will and Pete, he realized he needed a little more information before he could get started. After all, he didn't know the relationship between the pair.

Can Will be involved in a confidential conversation?

"Uh, we didn't really know each other well in college," Drew began slowly, meeting Will's gaze. "And you have different last names." He opened the file and tapped it. "Will I find documentation in here that I can discuss Pete's treatment in front of you, Will? Or do I need to ask you to leave?"

That was the last thing Drew wanted to do. He wanted to keep Will in view until he figured out a way to ask for the man's phone number. Still, he would do it for patient confidentiality reasons.

Please say you can stay.

ABOUT THE AUTHOR

Charlie started writing fantasy when she was eight, and after stumbling onto her first erotic romance at age nineteen, she realized her true calling. She now focuses on writing gay erotic romance, normally of the paranormal variety, with heroes of all kinds. With the help and support of her husband, Charlie finally fulfilled one of her life-long goals . . . move to acreage with her horses. You can often find her curled up with her laptop and a cup of tea or glass of wine, creating her next adventure. Charlie enjoys exploring the mountains of her new Oregon home on horseback, 4-wheeler, or motorcycle.

She can be reached at ch.richards2010@yahoo.com
Or visit her at www.charlie-richards.com

www.ingramcontent.com/pod-product-compliance
Lightning Source LLC
Chambersburg PA
CBHW070536130626
46555CB00003B/1457